A WAR THROUGH TIME!

DOCTOR ZEE: Why did you not tell me that Xaviar wanted to use my Time Warp synthesizer?
COMMANDER ADAMA: That maniac! We must bring him back!
DOCTOR ZEE: A chase through thousands of years of history! *That* should be interesting. You must be very, very careful, Adama—or that planet called Earth below us could disappear in a twinkling of an eye . . .

GALACTICA DISCOVERS EARTH!
The newest BATTLESTAR GALACTICA adventure

By GLEN A. LARSON AND MICHAEL RESNICK

BattlestaR
GALACTICA 5
GALACTICA DISCOVERS EARTH

NOVEL BY
GLEN A. LARSON AND
MICHAEL RESNICK

Based on the Universal Television Series
"Galactica 1980"
Created by Glen A. Larson
Adapted from the episodes
"Galactica 1980: Galactica Discovers Earth,
Parts I, II, and III"
Written by Glen A. Larson

B
BERKLEY BOOKS, NEW YORK

BATTLESTAR GALACTICA 5:
GALACTICA DISCOVERS EARTH

A Berkley Book / published by arrangement with
MCA PUBLISHING, a Division of MCA Inc.

PRINTING HISTORY
Berkley edition / December 1980
Second printing / September 1981
Third printing / November 1982

ISBN: 0-425-06125-6

A BERKLEY BOOK ® TM 757,375
Berkley Books are published by Berkley Publishing Corporation,
200 Madison Avenue, New York, New York 10016.
The name ''BERKLEY'' and the stylized ''B'' with design
are trademarks belonging to Berkley Publishing Corporation.
PRINTED IN THE UNITED STATES OF AMERICA

Part 1:

NOW

1

My sons are dead.

With Zac it came early. He was barely more than a boy. Apollo lived long enough to become our greatest warrior, to scatter the spaceways with the rubble of Cylon spacecraft, to even inspire fear in the brains of those loathsome creatures. But he is dead nonetheless, a millionth or a billionth or a trillionth victim of the Cylon Wars.

But the *Galactica*, that which my sons and so many others died to protect, still lives. It has been our home and our fortress for lo these many years, majestic and serene, strong and protecting, a haven and a hope and, yes, even a weapon.

And now, at last, it is nearing the end of its long, almost endless journey across the trackless wastes of space. Earth, that almost mythical blue and green world, is finally at hand.

I cannot tell anyone what hopes I have for this almost-forgotten world, what dreams she inspires, for fear of their disappointment should Earth turn out to be something less than expected.

But why should it be? Without continuous attacks by Cylon forces, what scientific wonders might they have wrought? Might they even have spawned a race of warriors against whom my own sons would have appeared puny and helpless? Might not they even have created an

3

Ultimate Weapon before which even the Cylons must bow down in defeat?

I envision Earth as a Utopia, where all men stand free and proud, where fear is so remote from their daily lives that even the meaning of the word has been lost in antiquity, an Earth where technology and religion have finally achieved a balance in the daily lives of its citizens, and where a benevolent government of and by the people has made the concept of Heaven a living breathing thing, a daily occurrence to each of its myriad members.

And yet, even as these thoughts cross my mind, there exists in the back of my brain a tiny, microscopic fear as well: will we appear as savages to them, so primitive as to be beneath their notice entirely? Will our Battlestar appear as nothing more than a children's toy to them, our hand weapons mere playthings?

For many years this uncertainty has been gnawing at the edges of my consciousness, the thought that they might have so far surpassed our civilization as to be almost a completely different species of a higher level.

And yet . . . and yet, they cannot be, for they are what we have spent so many years and so many young lives to reach.

We cannot do without them.

FROM DOCTOR ZEE'S DIARY TAPES:

I was silent as long as possible, since there was no valid reason to alarm anyone prematurely. But when I could wait no longer, I summoned Commander Adama to my chambers and explained the problem to him.

"When can we land?" he asked with the eagerness of a child, but the old, old eyes of a man who has been searching the heavens for Earth for too many years.

I decided to be blunt.

"We cannot land. Not now . . . and perhaps never."

I have not seen him look so shocked and stunned since the day Apollo died.

"But . . . but Doctor Zee," he stammered, shaking his head as if to clear it from a heavy blow, "What do I say? How can I tell these people who have come so far that their moment of triumph is to be denied them?"

"You will tell them what you must," I said.

"But Earth is ours! It stands before us!"

"No, Adama. It crawls before us, swathed in diapers and baby blankets."

"I don't understand," said Adama, starting to recover from his initial shock.

"Our tenacious pursuit of Earth has been founded on her ability to help us defeat our enemies," I said. "Is this not correct?"

He nodded.

"And it is a foregone conclusion that our enemies will become Earth's enemies, once the Cylons become aware of Earth?"

"Of course," said Adama. "But what is your point?"

"My point is simply this: I now believe we have visible proof that Earth is not advanced enough to help us."

"You mean militarily?" he asked.

"Militarily, scientifically, socially," I said gently. "In every way possible, they are ages—no, eons—behind us."

"It can't be!" said Adama.

"But it is."

"I need proof!"

"And so you shall have it," I said. "Look to the monitors."

FROM THE ADAMA JOURNALS:

It was frightening. Unbelievable yet undeniable. It so overloaded my senses that I still don't recall clearly all the things I saw. To aid in my memory, I am referring to the computer log:

Monitor Alpha: Twenty-two men in uniform faced

each other on a turf-like substance, eleven on each side. After an instant of immobility, a man at the center made a sudden motion and everything was thrown into disarray. Men of each side hit and pounded and tackled the others, some seemed to be beaten senseless, and finally a man in a striped shirt blew a whistle and the warfare stopped. But only momentarily. It began again and again, with gladiators from both side being helped from the field every few centons. And throughout this entire bloody battle, a quarter of a million people were cheering wildly. What savagery is this?

Monitor Beta: A man, simply clad, rode into a small, obviously poverty-stricken municipality on a strange-looking animal, dismounted, and walked down the middle of the major thoroughfare. Three men, each dressed more dismally than the next, walked forward to meet him. At what seemed to be a predetermined signal, all four reached for their hand weapons, which turned out to be extremely primitive projectile weapons. The lone man emerged victorious, threw a metal star-like object—obviously his insignia and rank—on the ground, spit on it, and rode away on his steed, which probably couldn't travel one hundred microns in a yahren. I can't believe it: projectile weapons, and an entertainment that glories in one man killing others of his own species!

Monitor Gamma: Metal vehicles careened down concrete thoroughfares, killing an occasional pedestrian without a second thought. The final vehicle in the parade, obviously belonging to a martial authority, was inhabited by men with no quicker reflexes nor better weapons (nor even nobler dispositions) than the first vehicle, which obviously carried a gang of lawbreakers.

Monitor Omega: Animation for children, with a story revolving about a bird and a furry carnivore. The carnivore kept trying to kill the bird (for food, or a blood feud—who knows?) and did enormous violence and damage to himself and the ecology, causing earthquakes to occur and volcanoes to explode. This cannot be what children watch! Even with such primitive, even primeval, technology, surely our values cannot be so different from our brethren on Earth.

Monitor Delta: Men with painted faces and ill-fitting clothes spent most of their time tripping one another and throwing food in circular pans in each other's faces. And everyone laughed!

Monitor Epsilon: A war entertainment, which was more instructive than all of the other monitors. Doctor Zee is indeed right: we must not lead the Cylons to Earth. One Cylon ship alone can destroy the planet, as impossible as that seems even now that I have had time to digest Earth's visual transmissions. The warriors have no force shields, no laser weapons, no individual protection except for some ill-fitting metal helmets. Their aircraft travel so slowly that it seems even a bird must be swifter. Their cities are open to attack, their defenses are nil, their offensive weapons are inaccurate and incredibly wasteful of ammunition. And worst of all, this recreation of war does not show them fighting against Cylons or some other enemy to the common cause, *but against themselves*!

What will become of Earth if the Cylons find her— and, whether they find her or not, what will become of *us*?

FROM DILLON'S LOG:

Everyone had heard rumors, but no one seemed to know what was going on. Earth was radioactive, Earth was deserted, Earth had been taken over by the Cylons, Earth was ready to help us, Earth was preparing to declare war on us, Earth was too advanced to be bothered with us, Earth was too primitive to help us. You paid your money and you took your choice. Me, I was betting on Earth being deserted. I figured they had been monitoring us for a few yahrens, had mounted a fleet, and were off to engage the Cylons. And, since they couldn't know the outcome for sure, they took the standard precaution of evacuating the planet so that if one of them were captured and tortured into revealing where Earth was, the Cylons wouldn't be able to kill any of his countrymen. I figured they were spread throughout the system, and maybe in a few neighboring solar systems as well.

It just goes to show you how useless rumormongering is.

I got a message to take Troy to the *Galactica*, which is when I figured out that maybe there was more to the situation than met the eye. After all, he could have monitored the meeting from the Colonial Freighter; if Doctor Zee and Commander Adama wanted the top-ranking warriors to meet them in person, something was up. We were either going to land immediately, or we weren't going to land at all. And if we *were* going to land immediately, why hadn't the news been piped over the various intercom systems? We've certainly been waiting for this moment long enough.

Troy didn't seem bothered at all. He's the youngest of the ranking warriors, but he's come by his rating honestly. With Adama and Apollo as his adoptive grandfather and father, he has had to prove time and again that his promotions were won strictly on merit and not because of influence. He proved it, all right— again and again, until it seemed that he had single-handedly raised the standard for excellence among our warriors.

Truly, he could have been the blood son of Apollo— though it took him a long time to get rid of the nickname of "Boxey" that had been hung on him. He told me once that it had to do with his being a fearsome little child. Well, his manners have improved, but he's still fearsome to his foes. To me, though, he's just a good friend: the best I've got. And I asked him, as one friend to another, what he knew about this meeting.

"Not a whole lot more than you do," he said, with a look that told me it would be only polite not to push him on the subject.

"All I want to know is if something's gone wrong," I persisted. "The way the rumors are flying . . ."

"You know better than to listen to rumors, Dillon," he said.

"Then we'll be landing soon?"

"I doubt it."

"Just what is the trouble?" I asked. I knew I shouldn't have pressed the point, but I couldn't help it.

"Oh, nothing much," he said with a smile. "Sometimes it's just bad manners to drop in unannounced."

Which got me to thinking.

We were only half a million miles away from Earth. How could they not know we were here?

TRANSCRIPT OF THE MEETING HELD IN
DOCTOR ZEE'S PRIVATE AUDITORIUM:

DOCTOR ZEE: And so we cannot land yet. Possibly we can never land. Should the location of Earth become known to the Cylons, it would surely mean the destruction of the planet.

COMMANDER ADAMA: But Doctor Zee, we haven't seen the forces of the Cylon Alliance for more than two yahrens.

DOCTOR ZEE: Only because they haven't wanted us to see them.

COMMANDER ADAMA: What are you saying?

DOCTOR ZEE: That they simply decided to let us lead them to the last remaining outpost of humanity in the Universe: the people of Earth.

COMMANDER ADAMA: Are you absolutely sure?

DOCTOR ZEE: Am I ever unsure?

COMMANDER ADAMA: Forgive me. But even now, the spectre of a fourteen-year-old boy with a mind a millennium ahead of its time . . .

DOCTOR ZEE: Adama, I have no false modesty about my intellect, since it was caused by a genetic accident rather than any effort on my part. The presence of a pure intelligence such as myself may prove disconcerting to some and frightening to others. I assure you that I am neither a freak nor a monster, but merely a fortuitous blending of chromosomes.

COMMANDER ADAMA: I'm not sure I understand what you're getting at.

DOCTOR ZEE: Don't resent my intelligence, Adama. *Use* it.

COMMANDER ADAMA: Forgive me, Doctor Zee. You have been in our midst for so long, and have been proven right so often, that I have no reason ever to doubt anything you say. I suppose it's the nature of the beast. I want so desperately for something to be true that I soon cause myself to believe it *is* true, regardless of the facts at hand.

DOCTOR ZEE: This is perfectly understandable, and I certainly bear you no malice for desiring proof of what I say. The proof can be found in the vicinity of Barnard's Star, which is a little more than six light-years distant from Earth.

DILLON: Barnard's Star? I'm not acquainted with it.

DOCTOR ZEE: It is the Terran name for it, just as "light-year" is another Terran term. I feel that, despite the problems confronting us, it would be best for us to start thinking in Earth terms whenever possible. This is especially so of those military lieutenants I have summoned to this room, as I shall explain before too long. But first, I think Commander Adama should brief you on the simpler physical aspects of Earth.

COMMANDER ADAMA: You all know that we have been searching for Earth for all these many years. But until recently it was just a name, a vague hope, a dream to be grasped at. We now know that Earth is the third of nine planets circling a class G-2 star known as Sol. Her proximity to the sun provides the only climate in this solar system, indeed on this spiral arm of the galaxy known as the Milky Way, capable of supporting life as we know it. Seven-tenths of the Earth's surface is covered by water, though that's nothing to worry about. There is plenty of room for all our people. The land masses are divisible into six habitable continents and there is a seventh one, totally frozen, at the planet's south pole. In addition, there are literally thousands of islands dotting the oceans. Twenty percent of the land masses are deserts and wastelands, unusable by Earth's inhabitants, but which our technology could easily reclaim and transform. There is, however, some disquieting news that makes immediate reclamation and settlement impossible. Doctor Zee, you have the floor.

DOCTOR ZEE: Thank you. But before discussing Earth, let me return to Barnard's Star for a moment. Not only is Barnard's Star devoid of life, but it—or rather the two gas giant planets that circle it—are incapable of supporting not only life as we know it, but indeed any type of life requiring an advanced technology.

TROY: Why is that, Doctor Zee?

DOCTOR ZEE: Because technology requires fire, and fire cannot exist without oxygen, and oxygen does not exist anywhere in the Barnard system.

XAVIAR: I begin to understand. You've discovered neutrino activity.

DOCTOR ZEE: Correction. There is always a certain amount of neutrino activity anywhere in the Universe. But there is far more than there should be in the vicinity of Barnard's Star, which can lead to only one conclusion: it is being caused by the power output of the Cylon fleet. Hence, it is logical to assume that they are waiting for us to lead them to Earth.

TROY: But won't our taking up orbit around Earth tend to convince them that we have indeed found what we were looking for?

DOCTOR ZEE: Yes. This is why I have ordered that the *Galactica* be taken out of orbit within ten hours and transported to the Centaurus system. Hopefully the Cylons will assume that we observed Earth for a few hours—another Terran term—and decided that this was not the planet we were seeking. From Centaurus we'll move to other stars, all in this broad general vicinity.

KIP: Why don't we simply enlist Earth's aid?

DOCTOR ZEE: I'm coming to that. If you will all watch Monitor Ceti closely, you will have your answer. What you are about to see will alarm you. However, I urge you to remain calm, for it is intended only to inform and educate you.

FROM THE MEMORY BANK OF
MONITOR CETI:

Scene 1: A tranquil, sunny day in Paris.

Scenes 2–5: Similar scenes of Los Angeles, New York, and London.

Scene 6: Los Angeles again.

DOCTOR ZEE (voice-over)*:* You have looked at some of the major cities of Earth. Now on screen is a megalopolis known as Los Angeles, in the United States of America, a nation composed of some fifty principalities.

DILLON (whispering)*:* What is that strange-looking brown haze blanketing the city?

TROY (whispering)*:* Must be a defense shield of some kind. Seems very mobile; it must be quite sophisticated.

DOCTOR ZEE: I'm afraid you are mistaken, Captain Troy, as you shall soon see. What you are observing is a 20th Century city of seven million people going blithely about their daily business.

TROY: Twentieth Century? I'm not sure I understand, Doctor Zee.

DOCTOR ZEE: It is a bit confusing, I'll admit. However, you must realize that the Lords of Kobol are not worshipped throughout the Universe. Earth has numerous different religions. Those who believe in the divinity of Jesus Christ, who lived some twenty centuries ago, date their calendars from his death. The Jews, to whose sect Jesus belonged during his lifetime, date their calendar back almost six thousand years. There are other sects, some more numerous than the Jews and Christians combined—the Moslems, the Hindus, the Buddhists, and a host of others—many of whom use their own dates. At this moment in Earth's history, the peoples of the northern hemisphere are the most technologically advanced, and so I find it convenient to use their terminology, since they represent the people we will be making contact with.

DILLON: I've been watching their vehicles . . .

DOCTOR ZEE: They're called automobiles.

DILLON: These automobiles sure don't move very fast.

TROY: On the other hand, they keep a nice neat formation. It must require a lot of practice and discipline. Notice those narrow painted lanes.

DOCTOR ZEE: Actually, you are watching a congested traffic jam on the Ventura Freeway. These automobiles form the Terrans' primary means of transportation, utilizing a primitive power mode known as an internal combustion engine.

DILLON: What does it do?

DOCTOR ZEE: It supplies motive power by burning a fuel known as gasoline, derived from petrochemicals . . . the decomposed matter of things that lived many eons ago in Earth's early history.

KIP: Seems useful.

DOCTOR ZEE: Actually, it's very inefficient and wasteful. And of course, the exhaust fumes pollute the atmosphere. That was the brown haze you noticed earlier, Dillon. But now, watch carefully.

Scene 7: An air raid siren rings out, and the pedestrians scurry about, looking confused.

Scene 8: Downtown Los Angeles. People flee every direction in a blind panic.

Scene 9: Cylon fighters appear overhead and begin strafing runs.

Scene 10: The streets of Los Angeles are littered with thousands of corpses. The city is in flames.

Scene 11: New York. The Empire State Building has had its top sixty stories sheared off by Cylon fighters, and the streets have been laid open to the subway level.

Scene 12: Paris. The Eiffel Tower lays on its side, having crushed some ten thousand people as it fell. Only gaping holes in the ground remain where once the world's greatest art treasures were stored in beautiful museums.

Scene 13: London. Big Ben has been demolished, London Bridge has collapsed into the Thames, Buckingham Palace is in flames. And, everywhere, are the bodies—scorched, twisted, agonized.

Scene 14: Over California. The Strategic Air Command has sent up a crack squadron of twelve jet fighters to do battle with the Cylons. One Cylon ship destroys the entire squadron in a matter of seconds. No damage is suffered by the Cylon forces.

Scene 15: The original fourteen sequences are run backward until everything is as it was.

TRANSCRIPT OF THE MEETING HELD IN
DOCTOR ZEE'S PRIVATE AUDITORIUM (Continued):

DOCTOR ZEE: No, the Earth has not been destroyed. What you have been watching was only a computer simulation of what *could* happen if we go ahead with our proposed landing on Earth.

COMMANDER ADAMA: It is Doctor Zee's contention that Earth is not yet capable of defending herself against our enemies. If we were to land at this point in Earth's history, we would bring death and destruction upon Earth as surely as if we attacked her ourselves.

XAVIAR: My dear Adama, and Doctor Zee—if we cannot go back because of a Cylon force behind us, and we cannot go forward because it would cause the destruction of the Earth, just what *do* we do? Simply give up?

DOCTOR ZEE: Not at all, Xaviar. As we lead the Cylon fleet away from Earth, we will simultaneously be working to bring Earth up to a level of technology whereby they can help us.

XAVIAR: And you think the Cylons are going to let us dupe them like this?

DOCTOR ZEE: I never make suppositions, Xaviar. I *know* the Cylons are going to let us dupe them like this.

XAVIAR: Even so, how does that bring Earth into our own century of technological development?

DOCTOR ZEE: I propose that in any case we should only bring her along slowly and unobtrusively, once we have decided who we can trust to help us rather than annihilate us.

COMMANDER ADAMA: Annihilate us?

DOCTOR ZEE: Yes. The video signals from Earth make it quite clear that it is an explosive planet whose warring factions could, in certain circumstances, be as dangerous as the enemy behind us.

COMMANDER ADAMA: Is there no one who can be expected to accept us?

DOCTOR ZEE: Let us say, rather, that there are precious few. You must understand that Earth is a primitive planet in every sense of the word. Two hundred years ago machines, except for a few that made war more efficiently, were unheard of. They have only had the power of flight—not space flight, mind you, but flight above the surface of their own planet—for three-quarters of a century. There is still strife between nations, between races, between religions. Even such incredibly basic things as the computer, the transistor, nuclear fusion, things such as that, have been known here for less than thirty years. There are many alive on Earth now who were fully grown before the first successful video transmission, known as television, was accomplished. You must at all times remember who and what we are dealing with.

COMMANDER ADAMA: But surely there must be a few visionaries amongst them?

DOCTOR ZEE: A few. There is even a field, recently created, in which these men and women tell their visions, couched in fictional form, known as science fiction. There have been some phenomenal minds at work here, writers named Wells and Verne and Heinlein and Asimov and Stapledon and Bradbury and Clarke, and to some extent they have paved the way for people to cast off their old perceptions of the Universe and to accept new ideas; but you must further understand that for every person whose mind is made more open by this form of literature, there are fifty who view it as mere entertainment and five thousand who have never read it. There have been very successful films—images preserved on celluloid and projected by light diffusion—on the likelihood of life on worlds other than the Earth, but the immense majority of the populace does not believe in this and is not ready to accept it.

XAVIAR: Are you not overreacting just a bit in this area, Doctor Zee? After all, once we land they will have no choice but to acknowledge the truth of our existence.

DOCTOR ZEE: Not true, Xaviar. Whatever country we make our presence known in will immediately assume we represent a nation with whom they are at war. They will clutch at fifty more comfortable explanations before they finally force themselves to face the truth, and by then we will have been killed, or will have been forced to kill them. Imagine a warrior without the precise ethical sense we drill into him, and you have a typical Earth inhabitant—or a typical Earth government, for that matter.

COMMANDER ADAMA: Then how do you propose that we enlist Earth's help?

DOCTOR ZEE: We will send down teams who will work without revealing themselves to the general population. In the beginning we will approach only certain members of Earth's scientific community, key men whom I have targeted as being in a position to accept us and our knowledge.

TROY: I thought you said that *none* of them would do that.

DOCTOR ZEE: And so I did. But these men will be in a unique position to evaluate certain information that no Terran could possibly give them, and will be forced, reluctantly but inevitably, to accept the truth. Each of the men I have chosen is relatively free of political ambition, and truly desires peace. Each, once he accepts it, will use our technology wisely. Are there any questions? Xaviar, you look dubious still. Have you any comment? No? Then this meeting is concluded. Landing parties will depart immediately.

CRUMPLED NOTE PAPER FOUND
IN XAVIAR'S QUARTERS:

Fools!
Fools!
FOOLS!

FROM THE ADAMA JOURNALS:

Once again I must send men I cherish off into the
unknown, in the service of the *Galactica*. I look at Troy,
and I can see nothing but Apollo. They are much alike:
the open face, the ready smile, the total confidence that
never quite crosses the border to bravado or foolishness.
And yet Apollo looked just that way—open, smiling,
confident—just before he left on the mission from
which he never returned. May the Lords of Kobol watch
over my grandson. So hopes his commander; so prays
his grandfather.

INTRASHIP REPORT:

When Doctor Zee had assembled the landing teams in
the fighter bay, he waited a moment until he had their
attention, and then spoke.

"Unhappily," he began, seeming as always to almost
glow with cerebral power as he spoke, "I have not had
time to prepare you for all you shall find on Earth. We
have endeavored to equip you and your languatron with
as much of Earth's slang and terminology and as many
of its customs as we could perceive from monitoring
their broadcasts. However, there will be gaps in your
knowledge which may very well expose you to danger.
My advice is to remember that all things in the Universe
are ultimately logical, and that it should be much easier
for you to disguise yourselves as semi-barbarians than it

would be for them to disguise themselves as civilized men.

"To aid you in your endeavor, I place in your keeping my latest innovation. As you all know, each color and sound has its own wavelength and frequency. Some of these are completely beyond the perception of the human eye and ear: colors beyond the infrared band, to use just one example.

"By generating a color combination in a frequency above the perception of Earth's conventional electronic equipment, and totally beyond the capabilities of the human eye, we can render equipment and personnel virtually invisible."

Doctor Zee took a device from the table before him.

"Watch closely," he instructed them, and pushed a button on the device.

The nearest Viper began to glow. It grew brighter and brighter, and then, suddenly, it vanished.

"Where did it go?" asked Lietuenant Dillon.

"Nowhere," smiled Doctor Zee. "The ship hasn't moved one iota. But, because I have encompassed it in a color field far beyond the frequency of the human eye, it can no longer be seen. To put it in simpler terms, an object that appears red is actually every visible color *except* red; red is the one color it reflects rather than absorbs, and hence red is what you see when you look at it. My device, to oversimplify, absorbs *all* colors into its high frequency field. You still look doubtful, Lieutenant Dillon; why not toss a cubit at the space where the ship was?"

Dillon did so, and was not surprised to see it apparently bounce off empty air.

"Unfortunately," continued Doctor Zee, "the energy necessary to generate such an aura around a Viper, or even around a single human form, is too great to sustain for any lengthy period of time. Hence, this device must only be used when absolutely necessary."

"Hiding from the people we've come to help," muttered Dillon.

"Are you sure," asked Troy, "that we can afford the time it will take to infiltrate Earth?"

."The cold hard truth is that there is no central government on Earth," said Doctor Zee. "There is no single leader with whom we can negotiate."

"If you say so then it must be true, Doctor Zee," said Troy, puzzled. "But I don't understand how they get together for their common good."

"The answer to that is quite simple," said Doctor Zee with a sad little smile playing about his perfect lips. "They don't."

Troy's jaw fell open.

"Each of you," announced Adama, "has a teammate, and each team has been programmed to go to scattered areas on Earth. Your entry patterns will bring you into Earth's atmosphere in unpopulated zones, and your navigational computrons will guide you over the safest possible routes toward population centers." He paused and looked at them, his keen eyes appraising the cream of the *Galactica's* young warriors. "Each of you will ultimately encounter the people of Earth. You have been briefed on how to conduct yourselves. May the Lords of Kobol watch over you."

TRANSMISSION FROM FLIGHT DECK:

TROY: Well, what do you think, Dillon?

DILLON: Piece of cake, to borrow a quote from an Earth transmission.

VOICE OF DOCTOR ZEE: May I remind you, Lieutenant Dillon, that even the best-planned cakes have been known to fall?

KIP: I wonder what a cake is, anyway?

2

UFO SIGHTED OVER LOS ANGELES!

(UPI) Police, Air Force and newspaper phones were ringing off the hook this afternoon as more than two thousand callers tried to report seeing two Unidentified Flying Objects over the greater Los Angeles metropolitan area.

Three different Air Force public relations officers have identified the objects as swamp gas, a low-flying commercial airliner, and meteorites.

This is the largest mass sighting since that which occurred over a South African army base some 22 years ago.

General Tucker Wilson, head of the Strategic Air Command, could not be reached for comment. His aide, Colonel Henry Beckworth Davies, denied any knowledge of either the reports or the UFOs themselves.

3

RECONSTRUCTED FROM
DILLON'S DEBRIEFING SESSION:

They were in trouble immediately.

No sooner had they entered the atmosphere over New Mexico than the S.A.C. base at Albuquerque picked them up on radar and sent two jet fighters after them. They tried out-maneuvering the fighters at Earth speeds, found that they couldn't escape, and finally had to go to their turbo boosters. The gambit worked, and they were soon thousands of miles away, but they had revealed far more about their capabilities than they wanted to.

They found themselves over the Atlantic, shot up into the stratosphere, and orbited the planet, coming down in power dives once they were over Los Angeles. They were spotted by literally thousands of civilians, but they landed so quickly that the military couldn't get a fix on them.

They found themselves in an empty field just before the Mojave Desert began in earnest. Troy got out of his ship, opened the cargo hold, and withdrew a two-wheeled vehicle that looked similar to the motorcycles that had been observed on Earth's video transmissions.

Dillon followed suit, and, pausing only long enough to flip a small switch that activated Doctor Zee's invisibility field, they mounted their bikes and were soon heading in the direction of downtown Los Angeles.

"I just hope no one comes galloping across that field and bumps into the Vipers," remarked Dillon as they turned onto a major highway.

"Don't worry about it," said Troy. "Earth people seem to congregate in cities. Those ships could sit there for years before anyone comes within a mile of them. We've got a more immediate problem on our hands."

"What?"

"There are about twenty ragged-looking men on motorbikes behind us."

"I don't see the problem," said Dillon.

"The automobile drivers haven't paid us much attention," explained Troy, "but bike riders might be able to spot significant differences between our vehicles and their own."

"What do you suggest?" said Dillon.

"No sense flying, or going at full speed," said Troy. "We've made enough dumb mistakes today. I suppose we'll just have to pretend that we belong here, and do our best to ignore them."

Which was easier said than done.

Donzo Gates was spoiling for a fight. He'd joined the Hell's Angels to see a little action, and except for a couple of gang wars things had been pretty quiet this month. Also, his old lady had been making eyes at Lizard Charlie all week, and he needed to do a little something to elevate himself in her eyes. Not that a guy who weighed some three hundred fifty pounds, all of it muscle and beard, should continually have to prove his merit, but that was the way the Angels worked. You not only had to claw and knife and gouge your way to the top, but you had to fight to stay there.

So when he saw the two weird-looking bikes up ahead, he decided to put a little life into an otherwise dull morning. Motioning Lizard Charlie and Billjac the Crusher to fan out, he spurted ahead, followed by a flying wedge of Angels.

Within minutes he had pulled even with Troy and Dillon.

"Hey, Lizard!" he hollered above the sound of the racing engines. "Get a load of those wheels!"

"Wild, man! Wild!" said Lizard Charlie.

"I sure would like one of them bikes for a toy!" yelled Billjac.

"No sooner said than done!" said Donzo. "Hey, you turkeys! Pull off the road. We've got to have a little pow-wow."

"You must have us confused with someone else," said Dillon. "My name's not Turkey, and neither is my friend's. In fact, as I recall, a turkey is a large, domesticated bird."

"A turkey is what I say it is, turkey!" snarled Donzo. "Now take the next exit ramp or I'm gonna crush your mush."

"Mush?" asked Dillon.

"Some form of warm cereal," said Troy. "It must be a slang expression."

"What do you think we should do?" asked Dillon, his hand poised above the turbo control.

Troy shook his head. "We've shown too much already," he said. "We'd better do what they ask."

Dillon shrugged and leaned his bike into the next exit ramp. A moment later he and Troy had come to a stop in a school playground, surrounded by twenty leering Angels.

Donzo dismounted and walked over to Troy's bike.

"Very nice wheels," he said. "You and I are gonna make a little trade, turkey."

"I appreciate your offer," said Troy apprehensively. "But we're already late for an appointment, and—"

"You didn't let me finish," said Donzo, giving him a shove. "I get to keep your bike. You get to keep your face. Fair trade?"

The Angels all laughed.

Troy sat stock-still, his brain racing, trying to come up with a way to avoid any type of conflict that might draw still further attention to himself and Dillon. But Donzo wasn't in the mood to wait, and pushed him again, nearly knocking him over.

"Is this the way you treat all strangers?" said Troy softly.

"Naw," chuckled Donzo. "Sometimes we ain't so friendly."

He reached out to give Troy another push, and the young warrior leaped into action. He grabbed Donzo's outstretched hand, twisted it behind the Angel's back, put a foot against the biker's buttocks, and pushed. Donzo uttered a surprised grunt, then fell head over heels and rolled to a stop at Lizard Charlie's feet.

"Not smart!" he hissed, pulling himself up and withdrawing a wicked-looking switchblade from his pocket. "Not smart at all, turkey!"

With a bellow he charged Troy again—and an instant later all three hundred fifty pounds of him were flying through the air. He hit the ground with a tremendous thud, and the force of the fall jarred the knife loose from his hand.

"Need a little help, Donzo?" asked Billjac the Crusher with an evil grin.

Donzo was too stunned to take offense. He merely nodded, and a moment later the two bikers were approaching Troy again, though much more cautiously this time.

"Now!" cried Donzo.

He raced forward, only to double over from a massive fist in his belly. Dillon, who had been standing quietly by, moved imperceptibly forward, grabbed Billjac by his beard, and flung him some fifteen feet away.

"We'd better end this quickly, Troy," he said. "Sooner or later someone from the school is going to see us."

Troy nodded, drew his weapon, set it on stun, and swept it over the remaining Angels, who collapsed as if an enormous block of concrete had fallen on them.

"What about these two?" said Dillon, indicating the still-prone Donzo and Billjac.

"Oh, I think all the fight is out of them," said Troy. "Bullies are pretty much the same anywhere in the Universe. However, let's make sure that they don't follow us too soon."

So saying, he picked up Donzo's knife and methodically slit the front tire of each of the Angel's bikes.

A few minutes later they were back on the highway again.

"Well, we haven't exactly been a smashing success so far," said Dillon. "Maybe it's the bikes."

"I doubt it," said Troy. "But just to be on the safe side, perhaps we'd better find some other means of transportation for the remainder of our trip. Let's take the next exit and see what we can find."

They pulled into a sleepy little town, left the bikes at the back of an empty lot, energized the invisibility field, and walked to a gas station.

"A telephone booth," mused Troy. "I seem to remember something about telephones in our briefing papers."

Dillon checked it out on his wrist computer. "Right. It's what they use to communicate with each other."

"Good," said Troy. "Then we can at least let Doctor Mortinson know we're coming."

Troy walked up to the phone, stared at it for a moment, then turned to Dillon.

"How does it work?"

"Strictly verbal, as I recall," replied Dillon.

"Fine." He stood about two feet from the receiver, cleared his throat, and spoke. "How do you do? I would like to communicate with the Pacific Institute of Technology."

Nothing happened.

"Maybe you have to speak louder," suggested Dillon.

Troy shrugged, repeated his request at the top of his lungs, and waited.

"Doctor Zee was finally wrong about something," said Dillon with a grimace. "It's not as easy to be a barbarian as he thinks."

"Let's loiter in the vicinity for a while until someone else uses it. Then we'll watch him and see how it's done."

Soon a middle-aged man pulled up to the station on a Harley-Davidson, took off his helmet, and rubbed his eyes.

"Whew!" he said. "Dusty out there! I just had to pull off the road for a moment to take a breather."

"Did you wish to use the telephone?" asked Dillon hopefully.

"Naw," said the man. "I just needed to rest for a minute."

"I mean, we wouldn't mind at all if you wanted to use it," continued Dillon hopefully.

"Why would I want to make a call?" said the man. "Besides, I need all my loot today."

"Loot?" repeated Troy blankly.

"Right. I'm going out to the track today. Putting it all down on Spectacular Bid."

"I'm afraid I don't follow you," said Dillon.

"Look, I know he couldn't beat Affirmed, and Affirmed couldn't beat Seattle Slew, but so what?" said the man. "I'm not saying he's the best thing that ever looked through a bridle. That's just hoopla to raise his syndication value. But there's nothing at Hollywood Park that can make him work up a good sweat, right? I mean, he's not racing the next Affirmed or Slew, just a bunch of hamburgers."

"Right," said Troy, nodding his head sagely and wondering what the man was talking about.

"And nine furlongs is his meat," said the man, starting his Harley up again. "Wish me luck. I'm putting the whole bankroll on him."

"Couldn't you just call it in by telephone?" asked Dillon hopefully.

"Some kidder!" laughed the man. He pealed out of the gas station.

"I don't think we've been properly prepared for contact," said Troy grimly. "I have absolutely no idea what he was talking about."

"Me neither," said Dillon. "At first I thought it might be the sport of horse racing, but hamburgers come from cattle, not horses. And what does hoopla mean? And if he doesn't work up a good sweat, does that mean he'll be working up a *bad* one?"

"Well, as long as we've got a minute, let's try the computer. Look up the word 'furlong'."

Dillon checked his wrist computer. "It's six hundred and sixty feet, two hundred and twenty yards, or one-eighth of a mile. Origin: the length of a farmer's furrow."

"Not exactly helpful," said Troy.

Suddenly he motioned Dillon into silence. A young woman had pulled up to a gas pump, left her car, and was approaching the phone booth.

"Uh . . . are you two using the phone?" asked Jamie Hamilton, brushing a lock of hair from her face.

"Oh, we're totally finished," said Dillon eagerly. "You can use it right now if you wish."

"You're sure?" she said, looking at them curiously.

"We have a considerable amount of communicating to do," said Troy hastily. "We can wait."

"Well, if you won't mind, I really am in kind of a hurry," said Jamie, entering the booth. "Thanks."

"Look at her, Troy!" whispered Dillon. "She's picking that thingamabob up and holding it next to her face. So *that's* the secret!"

"Oh, damn!" muttered Jamie to herself. "A toll call." She opened the door of the booth. "Do either of you have change for a dollar?"

Troy smiled pleasantly at her while Dillon checked his wrist computer.

"Sorry," he said, after checking the readout. "We have just used our last denomination of currency ourselves."

"You sure have a funny way of expressing yourself," said Jamie.

"We're from out of town," said Troy hastily.

"Oh, well. I'm going to get some change. Do you need any?"

"We'll be fine," said Troy.

"Credit card, huh? I wish I had one. The most important interview of my life, and I'm going to be late."

She scurried off to break a dollar at the station's cash register.

"This is hopeless," said Dillon. "I couldn't understand *her* either. It seems we can't get any currency until we contact Dr. Mortinson, and we can't contact Mortinson without currency."

"She said something about a card," noted Troy. "It's just possible that a sensor can read whatever these things work on."

"It's worth a try," agreed Dillon.

Troy removed his belt sensor, set it to "Read and Interact," aimed it at the phone, and waited. There was a momentary beeping, and then the coin box within the phone began spewing coins everywhere. The two warriors knelt down and began picking them up. They were still doing so when Jamie returned.

"What the hell are you doing?" she demanded.

"Just picking up our currency," said Dillon.

"Did you just jimmy that coinbox?" she persisted.

"No," said Troy. "It just started throwing these things—coins—out. I think it's malfunctioning."

"I'll just bet it is!" snapped Jamie. "And you looked like such nice, clean-cut young men. Hand that money to me and take a hike or I'll turn you in to the service attendant."

Dillon turned to Troy. "Metamorphosis? Transubstantiation? Boy, was Doctor Zee wrong about these people! Anyone who can turn me into a service attendant, whatever that is, has to be more advanced that we suspected."

"Hold on, now," said Troy. "She's not wearing any power units. Probably it's just another figure of speech."

"What are you talking about?" said Jamie, her eyes wide.

"Oh, nothing," said Dillon. "We just like to talk. Here's your currency." He handed a few hundred coins to her.

"We're strangers here," said Troy slowly. "We want to respect your customs, and we don't mean anybody any harm."

"I can believe you're strangers," said Jamie at last. "I'm just trying to figure out where you can come from that doesn't have any telephones."

"Oh, you've probably never heard of it," said Dillon hastily. "Would you care to use the phone now?"

"No," she sighed. "It would only look worse if I called in now. Maybe I can just give them an excuse about being stuck in a traffic jam."

"You're sure?" said Dillon. "We wouldn't mind your making a call at all."

"Thanks a lot," said Jamie dryly. "I'm still trying to decide what to do about you two."

"Just wish us luck;" said Dillon. "We're late for an appointment ourselves." He paused, then his face lit up. "Say, is there any chance that you'd be going anywhere near the Pacific Institute of Technology?"

"*That's* where you two are going?" said Jamie unbelievingly.

"Yes," said Troy. "We're going to see Doctor Mortinson."

"Doctor *Alfred* Mortinson?"

"Yes."

"*The* Doctor Alfred Mortinson?"

"There's more than one?" asked Dillon apprehensively.

"The nuclear bigwig, right?"

Troy nodded. "Yes. We had difficulty with our transportation."

Jamie stared at the two men for a long minute. "Well, maybe I did jump to conclusions. But you'll have to admit it did look a little odd."

"I *knew* it!" exclaimed Dillon. "I just knew we looked too different. That's why that guy with the knife tried to pick a fight!"

"What?" said Jamie. "Somebody attacked you with a knife?"

"No problem," said Troy. "It's all over."

"But you should report it to the police."

"On a telephone?" asked Dillon dubiously.

"Of course on a— Look, I can't stand here talking any longer. I'm really late. Hop into my car and I'll give you a lift."

"It flies, too?" asked Dillon, climbing into the back seat.

Jamie forced herself to laugh, then gunned the engine and began counting the moments until she could unload these two pleasant but unquestionably demented young men.

4

(AP) Anti-nuclear activists have received permits to demonstrate throughout California this afternoon. Among their major targets are the nuclear power plant to the north of San Francisco, and the Pacific Institute of Technology in the Los Angeles area. Security at the latter location has been increased following the reports of threats against the life of Nobel Prize laureate Alfred Mortinson.

5

It was a half-hour drive to the Pacific Institute. When they arrived Dillon and Troy were amazed to see hundreds of people, many of them teenagers but quite a few adults as well, marching around the campus carrying signs and placards.

"What seems to be the problem here?" asked Troy.

"See for yourself," said Jamie. "Your friend Mortinson may have invented a newer and safer nuclear power plant, but it's obviously not safe enough for these guys. Look at their placards."

NO NUKES IS GOOD NUKES	DON'T MAKE THE SNOW GLOW	BAN THE BURN
	MORTINSON, KEEP OUT OF OUR LIVES!	

"Clean and safe nuclear power—that's what this is all about?" said Troy.

"Isn't that enough?" said Jamie.

"I guess so. Anyway, thanks; you've been very kind."

"Strangers in a new place have to stick together," said Jamie. "If you ever want to get in touch with me, I'll be working at United Broadcasting . . . I hope."

"You hope?" said Dillon.

"That's the appointment I'm late for: a job interview."

Troy and Dillon thanked her again and got out of the car. As she drove off, one of the protesters picked up a rock and hurled it at her car, missing it by only a few yards.

"I don't like the looks of this, Troy," said Dillon.

"I do," replied his companion. "It tells us what Mortinson needs from us. We can turn him into a hero before the week is out."

Troy walked over to one of the demonstrators.

"Excuse me, friend, but can you tell us where we can find Doctor Alfred Mortinson?"

"See that big building over there," was the answer, "the one with all the cops around it?"

"Thanks," said Troy.

"They won't let you near it," said the demonstrator. "They've been busting skulls all day."

Troy smiled politely and began walking in the opposite direction from Mortinson's building.

"Wrong way, Troy," said Dillon.

"We've had enough confrontations today, Dillon. Let's see if we can't insinuate our way inside instead of just charging ahead."

"These clothes Doctor Zee gave us seem to go better with motorbikes than nuclear labs," said Dillon. "I don't know how you propose to get in without being challenged."

"I noticed what seems to be a storm sewer system beneath the streets," said Troy. He waited until he was sure no one was looking, then lifted a large grate from the pavement and lowered himself carefully into the darkness. "I was right," his voice echoed hollowly.

"Get a fix on the building with your computer and remember to put the grating back after you get down here."

A moment later they were walking beneath the campus, up to their ankles in water, their steps making strange sloshing noises.

"Reminds me of one of the ventilation shafts aboard the *Galactica*," said Dillon. "Except for the water, that is."

"I wonder if the other teams are having any better luck adjusting to the local customs," said Troy as they followed the computer's directions. "I know Kip was sent to someplace called the Union of Soviet Socialist Republics."

"He's probably accomplished his mission already," said Dillon. "This nation seems particularly paranoid. I'll bet Kip's people don't have all these security measures."

"Don't bet on it," said Troy. "This whole planet's got security on the brain. No one seems to trust anyone."

"Except for Jamie."

"Jamie?"

"The girl who drove us here," said Dillon.

"I don't know. I got the idea she was humoring us. Probably thought we were madmen who might get violent at any minute."

Dillon shrugged. "Who knows? Well, here we are. According to the computer we're right under the building."

"See anything that looks like a doorway?" asked Troy.

Dillon shook his head. "No such luck."

Troy pulled his sensor off his belt and pointed it directly above his head. Then he began walking in ever-widening circles. "All right," he said at last. "There are no life forms of any kind above where I'm standing. It seems to be a storage room, or perhaps an office. At any rate, the door is closed, which means we won't be seen."

He pulled out his weapon and fired it directly above his head, then jumped back as debris started tumbling down.

When the hole he was creating was large enough, he holstered his weapon and jumped up, grabbing the edges with his hands and easily pulling himself up. He reached down for Dillon's hand and hoisted his friend effortlessly.

"Looks deserted," he said, looking around him at an array of dust-covered file cabinets.

"Wait a minute," said Dillon, closing his eyes to concentrate better. "Right! As I recall, many Earth buildings have lower levels called basements, where the foundations—moorings, so to speak—are laid. That must be where we are."

"Good," said Troy. "Now if we can find an elevator, we can avoid the main level of the building altogether. Security shouldn't be anywhere near as heavy on the upper levels."

"But we still don't know exactly where Mortinson's office is located," said Dillon.

"We'll ask," said Troy.

"Just like that?"

"Why not? Once we're above the ground level, anyone who sees us will assume that we have a right to be there."

"Well, let's skulk around and see if we can't find some means of getting up there."

And as they spoke, Alfred Mortinson, Ph.D., Nobel Prize winner, husband and father, stood at a window some four floors above them, looking down at the protesters. He was a lean man, with thick curly hair, a generous moustache, and thoughtful, intelligent, sensitive eyes.

"How do we make them understand?" he muttered, more to himself than his secretary, a pert blonde named Carlyle who sat at her desk. "How do we impress upon them that you don't throw the baby out with the bathwater? That you don't give up on nuclear energy just because we don't have all the answers yet."

"Don't let them get to you like this, Doctor," said Carlyle soothingly.

"How can I ignore them?" he said in exasperation. "There may be a few kooks out there, but most of them are rational people with rational fears for their families. Even a rabble-rouser like Jane Fonda truly cares. She and they may be wrong, but I don't question their sincerity. They don't want their kids to glow in the dark, they don't want their city to blow sky-high. My God, do they think I do?"

"Sir . . ."

"Can't they understand that we have to move forward? The Wright brothers didn't just wake up one morning and say, 'Let's fly out to Kitty Hawk.' Doctors didn't just look at bread mold and say, 'Hey, let's make up a batch of penicillin.' We've only been in the Nuclear Age for a third of a century. Of course we don't have all the answers. I don't know how to break down nuclear waste, how to neutralize it, how to make it harmless. But I do know that there won't be a drop of oil anywhere in the world twenty-five years from now, and that I won't come up with the answers any faster because of a mob that likens me to another Baron von Frankenstein!"

He shook his head, then turned to Carlyle. "Do you think I ought to invite a few of them in, just to kind of sit around and explain what we're trying to do here?"

"They didn't come to listen," said Carlyle.

"No, I suppose not," said Mortinson. He looked out the window again. "I understand their concern. Why the hell can't they understand that?"

Suddenly a rock crashed through the window. Mortinson screamed, clutched his face, and fell to the floor. Carlyle raced to the window, drew the curtains shut, and knelt down beside him.

"Are you hurt badly?" she asked.

He touched his head gingerly, then looked at his hand, which was covered by far less blood than he had feared.

"Just a couple of cuts above the temple," he said.

"They probably look a lot worse than they are. I'm going down the hall to the washroom and treat them. You call someone up here to clean up the mess—and don't open the curtains."

"I'm also calling for the police," said Carlyle emphatically.

"You'll do no such thing," said Mortinson. "We've got enough problems without inciting a riot. Don't go overreacting."

"But . . ."

"Look, I've got to check my hair for slivers of glass. Just go back to work and try not to get too upset."

He walked out the door, leaving her looking apprehensively at the drawn curtains.

And, thirty-eight feet below them, Dillon and Troy were also glancing apprehensively at some window curtains.

"I don't see why not," Dillon was saying. "We've got suction holds for our hands and legs. It would be so *easy* to go out the window, climb the side of the building, and enter a few floors up."

"And if we're seen?" said Troy.

"We won't be. I peeked out. This is the back of the building. All the kids are around the front."

"Too risky," said Troy. "It only takes one person, and we're likely to get shot down without ever knowing what hit us. And, more important, we've got equipment on us that we just can't afford to have fall into their hands at this time."

"So what do you suggest?"

"Well, no one's in the room above us, according to my sensor. Let's put another hole in the ceiling and play it by ear."

Dillon shrugged, and a moment later Troy had blown a hole three feet wide into the basement ceiling. He pulled himself up gingerly, then froze.

"Something wrong?" asked Dillon.

"Made a mistake," Troy whispered. "This isn't a room. It's a main corridor. It's empty now, but—"

"HALT!" cried a voice.

"Oh-oh!" muttered Dillon.

Troy finished pulling himself up, then turned to face two blue-uniformed security men.

"Freeze!" snapped the nearer of them, leveling a gun at the young warrior.

Troy stood relaxed, his hands at his sides.

The second security man raced up and shoved him to the side of the corridor, face-first.

"Take the position, buddy!" he said harshly.

"The position?" asked Troy.

"Up against the wall, Mac!"

He placed Troy's hands and feet where he wanted them, then began frisking him.

"Hey, Scott, this guy's loaded for bear!"

"What's he got there?" said the cop named Scott.

"Some kind of hand weapon, and a lot of miniaturized electrical equipment."

"It's not electrical," said Troy calmly. "Please handle it carefully. It's quite dangerous."

"Look at that hole in the floor!" exclaimed Scott. "I'll say it's dangerous!"

"Okay, fella!" snapped his companion. "Suppose you come along with us. We've got a lot to talk about."

"I'd like to oblige you," said Troy, "but I have urgent business with Doctor Mortinson."

"Maybe he can arrange to come to your trial," said Scott.

The two security men suddenly became aware of a sharp whistling behind them.

"Do you guys really want to see how these things work?" asked Dillon, who had moved a chair beneath the hole and was standing on it, his head, arms and upper torso now visible to the security men. In his hand he held a strange-looking weapon.

"Good God! Another one!" said Scott. He reached for his pistol, but collapsed long before he could pull it from its holster. His companion followed him an instant later.

"I hope that was only set on stun," said Troy, retrieving his equipment from the unconscious men.

"Of course," said Dillon. "Boy, these guys have got a long way to go before they're ready to take on the Cylons."

"Just in the area of technology," said Troy. "There's nothing wrong with their courage."

"Well, we'd better not just stand here talking," said Dillon. "Let's get on with it."

Troy walked up and down the corridor until he came to an office listing on one of the walls. "Mortinson's in Room 408," he announced. "This must be the first floor. I have a feeling that we'd better try a stairway; they'll be less well-guarded than the elevators from what I've seen."

Dillon nodded, and they began searching for a set of stairs. They passed an EXIT sign four times before Troy thought of opening the door and finally found a stairwell. "Good," he muttered, stepping through and pulling the door shut behind Dillon. "How much longer will those two guys remain unconscious?"

"I don't know," said Dillon. "It should be about twenty minutes total, but I don't know how long we've been looking for these stairs."

"Then we'll just have to talk fast," said Troy, taking the stairs two at a time. He got off at the fourth floor and walked to a door marked:

408

ALFRED MORTINSON

Private

They entered, again swiftly closing the door behind them.

"Are you here to clean up the mess?" asked Carlyle, looking up from her typewriter.

"Mess?" asked Dillon.

"We've come to see Doctor Mortinson," said Troy.

"You and five hundred other freaks," said Carlyle. "How did you get up here?"

"It's very important," persisted Troy. "Possibly life and death."

"Who are you?" asked Carlyle, scrutinizing them carefully. "Does the Doctor know you?"

"We know the Doctor from a recent speech he delivered on what I believe you call your educational transmission band."

"Transmission band?" repeated Carlyle. "What are you talking about?"

"Television station," put in Dillon quickly.

"Right," agreed Troy.

"Well, I'm afraid this is a bad time to come in unannounced," said Carlyle. "As you can see, we're under a great deal of stress."

"I can see where it might make it difficult to theorize," said Troy, walking over to a desk computer that was tied in to a video screen. On the screen was a six-line formula keyed to an advanced binary identification system.

"Especially abstract theories of nuclear waste degeneration," agreed Dillon. "I had trouble with that theory myself. Look at that fourth line, Troy; he doesn't begin to understand how to accelerate the half-life of plutonium, or how to degrade his uranium isotopes."

"He's on the right track, though," said Troy.

"Look," said Carlyle, rising from her desk and confronting them. "I don't know who you are, but this isn't funny any longer. You know how Sherlock Holmes said that Moriarty had done a mathematical treatise that was so complicated that no one in the world was capable of criticizing it? Well, there aren't two other men who can understand Doctor Mortinson's work in its entirety, and that includes his own staff. So just what do you think you're pulling?"

Troy was about to answer when the phone rang, and Carlyle crossed the room to lift up the receiver.

"How do you make it ring?" whispered Dillon, whose pride was still smarting from his inability to make the telephone at the gas station respond to his needs. "That's got to be the answer. Make it ring, and then you can communicate!"

Troy gestured him to silence and went back to studying the readout on the video screen, as Carlyle tried not to appear too excited by what she was hearing.

"Right, Miss Carlyle," said the voice at the other end of the line. "This is Scott Miles of security. Two young men have just broken into the building. If they're in there with you now, just say, Good morning, Scott."

"Good morning, Scott," said Carlyle.

"All right," said Miles. "That's all we need to know. Now, try not to be alarmed. We're on our way. Have they revealed any weapons yet?"

"No."

"Good. We don't think you're in any immediate danger. We're pretty sure it's the Doctor they want, and we've got him in a safe place. Just let them think he's on his way, and move to the west corner of the room away from the door. Do you understand?"

"Completely," said Carlyle. "And thank you for calling."

She hung up the phone and turned back to Troy and Dillon. "The Doctor is on his way and should be here in just a couple of minutes," she said. "Can I get some coffee for you?"

She moved to the corner of the room just a little too quickly. Troy cocked an eyebrow, Dillon tried to hide a grimace.

"I'm afraid we can't stay," said Troy. "But we'd like to leave the Doctor a message." He walked to the keyboard. "The symbols are a little different from those I'm used to, but using the projection on the screen as a common cipher, I think we can give you the rudiments of something that might interest the Doctor."

Troy's fingers began hitting keys with the speed of a professional typist. Carlyle uttered a scream and raced across the room to stop him, but Dillon grabbed her and held her gently but firmly away.

"What are you doing?" demanded Carlyle, a note of panic in her voice. "Please! The Doctor has been working on that formula for three years!"

Troy hit an erase button, and the fourth and fifth lines of the formula disappeared. He then entered two very complex substitute lines.

"That should be enough," he said to Dillon. Then, to Carlyle: "Tell him he can reach us through a young lady named Jamie Hamilton at the United Broadcasting Corporation."

They walked to the door.

"Wait!" screamed Carlyle, nearly hysterical. "Please stay! He's on his way up!"

Troy and Dillon raced to the stairwell and walked down a quick two flights, then stopped to consider their next move.

"We can't just leave," said Dillon. "After all, the whole point of our mission was to get the Doctor on our side."

"They'll never let us near him," said Troy. "This place is under siege."

"But if he doesn't understand our message . . ."

"He'll understand it, all right," said Troy confidently. "No one now living on Earth could have finished that formula for him."

"You've got a funny expression on your face, Troy," said Dillon suspiciously. "What's on your mind?"

"There's one place we could go where Doctor Mortinson wouldn't have any trouble finding us. After all, Jamie may not get the job, so we can't really count on his being able to get in touch with us through her."

"I have a sinking feeling I know what you're going to suggest," said Dillon.

"Jail," nodded Troy.

"I knew it!" groaned Dillon.

"Why not?" said Troy. "The news media will cover it, Mortinson's secretary will identify us, and he'll know where to find us."

"And what if he doesn't want to?"

"Nonsense," said Troy. "Anyone who can work on that formula, and get as far as he got with the limited information available to him, has got to have too much curiosity imbedded in him *not* to see us. And besides, we can always escape from jail."

"We can, eh?" said Dillon. "I wonder. You know, we have continually underestimated the capabilities of

Earth people. They almost shot us down the second we got here, and we've been racing from one disaster to another ever since.''

"Have you got a better suggestion?" said Troy.

"Damn it!" said Dillon. "I *knew* you were going to ask me that. I just knew it!"

"Good. Then it's settled."

And so two warriors from the great ship *Galactica*, warriors who between them had destroyed more than seven hundred Cylons and almost as many of their ships, suddenly emerged on the main floor of the Pacific Institute of Technology and surrendered to authorities without striking a blow in their own defense.

6

Doctor Mortinson got back about two minutes after the cops arrested those two crazy men. He had a large bandage on his forehead, just above the temple, and though he shrugged it off, I guessed that they'd taken a couple of stitches to close the wounds.

"What was all the commotion?" he asked. "I just saw the police taking a pair of young men into custody."

"It's a good thing you weren't here," I said. "I think they must have been some kind of terrorists. I know they were looking for you."

I knew I was going to have to tell him sooner or later about the theory, but I was kind of hoping he'd be so upset that he'd go home first. Not that I was afraid, but I just thought he'd had a hard enough day as it was.

But after a moment of sitting at his desk, he got up and went back to the video readout screen, like he's done maybe five thousand times in the past year.

I had shut it off after those hoodlums destroyed what was there, and the Doctor quickly turned to me and questioned me about it.

"I'm afraid one of those freaks the cops arrested got to the keyboard and ruined it. I took it off the screen."

"My God!" he thundered. "Three years of work down the drain!"

43

"I tried to stop them!" I protested. "Really I did."

"I'm sure you did, Carlyle," he said, struggling to regain his composure.

"They kept talking as if they understood what it meant," I continued. "Talking about half-lives and such. You wouldn't have believed their gall."

"I hope you didn't erase it completely," said the Doctor. "Perhaps I can salvage something from it."

"No," I said, glad to be able to give him some good news, no matter how small. "It's in the memory bank. But I don't think it's going to be of any use to you, sir. He ruined it. I really would have stopped him, but the security guards warned me to leave them alone."

"I don't hold you responsible," he said in a tired voice. "Please throw the formula, or what's left of it, on the screen."

I did so, and he stared at it, as if he'd never seen it before. Then he took out a pocket calculator and began pressing buttons like crazy.

And while he was playing with his computer and staring at the formula, his face, which at first had been merely irritated, took on the oddest expression. His eyes widened until I could see the whites all around the irises, and his jaw kind of hung slack. Finally he put his calculator back in his pocket and just gaped at the screen.

"My God . . ." he muttered.

"I'm sorry," I said consolingly. "I told you they ruined it."

He turned to me with a wild look in his eyes. At first I thought losing the formula had unhinged him, that he had completely lost his reason, but then he began speaking and his voice, though incredibly tense, sounded quite sane.

"Miss Tabakow," he said, using my last name for the first time in years, like he was so excited he had forgotten that he always called me Carlyle, "I want you to think very carefully. Who did these two men say that they were?"

"They didn't," I said, flustered. "I could tell that

they were just part of that street gang out there. Leather jackets, Levis, nothing special at all about them. Their hair was a little shorter and a little better groomed than most of the others, but that's the only difference I could tell. Really, Doctor, they were just a couple of hood-lums."

He shook his head irritably. "*Think*!" he snapped. "They must have said *something*!"

And then I remembered. "They said something about seeing you on PBS."

"PBS?" he repeated, a strange light coming over his face.

"Yes, sir," I said quickly. "Something about reading a paper on PBS. But they didn't call it that; they called it an . . . an educational transmission band."

"Of course they would call it that," he said, nodding to himself, as if I weren't even there. "And to think that they got this far without drawing undue attention! They had to master our language, our customs, even our road maps! And that PBS broadcast was a round-robin discussion I had with Carl Sagan and Adrian Barry about the possibilities of life elsewhere in the galaxy. But why me? Carl's always been a proponent of life on other worlds. I'm a Johnny-come-lately to the fold." He lowered his head in thought for a moment. "Of course! The formula! They could prove who they were to me in a matter of seconds; it could have taken days or weeks to convince Carl!"

I couldn't understand what he was talking about. I mean, after all, the problem was that these two crazies had messed up years of work, and here he was acting like they had done him a favor.

"Did they give any indication of how I can contact them?" he said at last.

"They're in jail," I said. "If you really want to see them, why not just go down to the station?"

"No jail can hold them . . . unless they want to be held," he said, saying the latter half of the sentence while staring off into space again. "No," he said, coming back to earth again. "They'd give themselves more than one opportunity. Think hard, Miss Tabakow: did they say anything else?"

And then I remembered. "Well, they did say you could get in touch with them through someone called Jamie Hamilton at the United Broadcasting Corporation."

"Well, don't just stand there!" he said, the faraway look gone from his eyes again. "Get this Hamilton person on the phone at once!"

"If you wish," I said. "But I can't imagine why you are so interested in a couple of hoodlums."

He gave me the strangest smile.

"These hoodlums, as you call them," he said, enunciating each word carefully, as if measuring its length, breadth and weight, "may be as important to mankind as the coming of the Messiah."

So I made the call for him, and went to the ladies' room to straighten up a bit, and when I came back he was gone.

So now I'm wondering: what's the good of job security when your boss goes off the deep end?

7

DISTRICT POLICE BLOTTER:

Name: Troy (Last name unknown)
Height: 6 feet, 4 inches
Weight: 194
Hair: Brown
Eyes: Brown
Distinguishing features: *No fingerprints!*
Offense: Breaking and entering, vandalism, assaulting two security men, causing structural damage to Pacific Institute of Technology.

Name: Dillon (Last name unknown)
Height: 6 feet, 3 inches
Weight: 202
Hair: Brown (light)
Eyes: Brown
Distinguishing features: *No fingerprints!* Scar on upper left arm of unknown origin; seems neither surgical, nor caused by any weapon on record. (Subject mentioned something about a "Sylon" or "Cylon" attack, but would say nothing further.)
Offense: Breaking and entering, vandalism, assaulting two security men, possibly caus-

ing structural damage to Pacific Institute of
Technology.

Bail for Troy Doe and Dillon Doe: None, until
accurate identification has been achieved.

8

Jamie showed up, flustered and breathless, and was led to the outer office of Dana Anderson, the West Coast News Director of the United Broadcasting Corporation.

It was an impressive anteroom, the walls covered by numerous plaques and certificates, awards for news-gathering excellence. Interspersed with these were photos of Anderson shaking hands with Presidents Carter, Nixon, Ford, Johnson and Kennedy; Governors Reagan, Brown the Elder, and Brown the Younger; and a host of Senators and Representatives. All were autographed, usually with a personal and friendly inscription. There was even a shot of a very dishevelled Anderson interviewing Don Drysdale after he had pitched fifty-four consecutive scoreless innings for the Los Angeles Dodgers.

She was properly impressed.

A young, well-built, but somehow prissy-looking woman came out of Anderson's private office.

"Miss Hamilton?" she said.

"Ms. Hamilton," corrected Jamie.

"Whatever," said the woman, slightly irritated. "I am Mr. Anderson's personal secretary. You are almost two hours late for your appointment."

"I know," said Jamie. "I had a flat tire, and got

caught in a jam behind an accident on the expressway, and . . .''

"I didn't ask you *why* you were late," said the woman. "I merely pointed it out. To be quite blunt, Ms. Hamilton, there are several people competing for the on-camera reporting job."

"I'm sure there are," said Jamie with more confidence than she felt, "but I intend to get it."

"We'll see," said the secretary primly. The phone rang and she picked up the receiver. "Yes," she said, staring curiously at Jamie. "She is. Who may I say is calling? We don't ordinarily take personal calls for non-employees here. *Who*?" Her glasses, balanced precariously on her upturned nose, almost fell off.

She handed the phone over to Jamie. "It's Mortinson. The man from the Pacific Institute. Why does he want to speak to you?"

"Hello?" said Jamie hesitantly.

"Miss Hamilton? This is Alfred Mortinson."

"Yes?"

"It is most urgent that I know more about those two friends of yours who came to my lab."

"Friends? I don't know what you're talking about."

"Please," said Mortinson. "There's no time for coyness. I assure you I am sympathetic to your cause."

"My cause?" repeated Jamie. "I'm afraid I don't under—" She broke off as her eyes fell on a television set and she saw news films of the police leading Troy and Dillon into custody.

"Oh, my God!" she said. "Doctor, I assure you, I had no idea that they were going to cause trouble."

"You don't understand," said Mortinson. "I'm grateful for their visit. In fact, I was hoping that you might be one of them."

"One of them?" asked Jamie. "One of whom?"

"They left your name as a point of contact. I had hoped to learn more from you before confronting them at the police station. Believe me, I bear them no malice. Quite the contrary."

"I'd like to tell you about them, Doctor Mortinson,

but I don't think what I know would be worth your while. They were very strange young men. Highly articulate and mannered, but they didn't even know how to use a telephone. If you want my opinion, they're just a couple of deeply weird characters.''

As she was speaking, Dana Anderson, tall, graying, his eyes flashing, entered the room and pulled his secretary aside. "Doctor Mortinson?" he whispered. She nodded. "*The* Doctor Mortinson? What the hell is he calling us for? He hates the press."

"He's not calling us," came the answer. "He's calling *her*."

"Who is she?"

"An applicant for the reporting job. She was two hours late."

Anderson quickly crossed the room, put his hand over the receiver, and whispered to Jamie: "See if you can meet him."

"But it's not what he thinks," protested Jamie.

"You want a crack at that job?" hissed Anderson. "Tell him you'll meet him."

As Jamie arranged an appointment with Mortinson, Anderson picked up another phone, pressed an in-house button, and began arranging for a mobile unit, a top cameraman, and a mini-mike.

Jamie hung up at last and turned to Anderson. "Well, I did what you said, not that it'll do much good."

"You just do the interviewing," said Anderson. "I'll decide what good it is."

"Does this mean I've got the job, Mr. Anderson?"

"You get us an interview with Mortinson and you're on salary the second he starts talking," said Anderson. "Where are you meeting him?"

"Outside police headquarters," said Jamie. "But really, sir, I'm doing this under false pretenses. I don't have the slightest idea who those two guys were."

"Guys?" said Anderson. "What guys? Oh, hell, never mind, it doesn't matter. All that counts is that we've finally found someone Mortinson will speak to.

Honey, you pull this off and I promise I'll sign you to a thirty-six-month contract. Fair enough?"

"You bet," said Jamie, looking forward to a routine question-and-answer session with the mysterious Doctor Mortinson.

It may have been under false pretenses, but there sure couldn't be any easier way to get a job.

9

XAVIAR: Adama, your grandson was to have reported in long ago. We've heard from all the other teams.

ADAMA: Be patient, Xaviar. Anything could have happened.

XAVIAR: Exactly. The folly of this plan is that it is so desperately dangerous. Doctor Zee must have become unbalanced to have conceived it.

ADAMA: Keeping Earth hidden from our enemies is not only in Earth's best interests, but our own as well.

XAVIAR: I'm not debating that. But we have better ways.

ADAMA: Such as?

XAVIAR: Such as a tool we have sought for generations and now possess, thanks to our young genius.

ADAMA: You're referring to the Time Warp Synthesizer?

XAVIAR: I am.

ADAMA: I cannot agree with you. The concept of time travel is dangerous at best, and possibly suicidal.

XAVIAR: But Adama, what could be more vital to Earth's survival than to speed up her civilization?

ADAMA: How? By going back into her past and

53

introducing scientific advances and knowledge centuries ahead of its time?

XAVIAR: Think of where they could be now!

ADAMA: I *am* thinking about it. I'm also thinking about the Snowball Effect.

XAVIAR: Snowball Effect? What is that?

ADAMA: It's inherent in Doctor Zee's equations. It states that changing a single incident in Time will have a cumulative effect on the present. For instance, you go back into Earth's prehistory and inadvertently step on a beetle. Just something as seemingly harmless as that. Except that a bird that would have eaten the beetle now flies elsewhere for food, and a carnivore that would have eaten the bird now eats a prehistoric man instead, and that man does not live to invent the wheel, and the whole of human history is changed.

XAVIAR: Preposterous!

ADAMA: Hypothetical, yes. Preposterous, hardly.

XAVIAR: Let me find out the truth. I'll take an expedition into Earth's past. We'll introduce electronics, atomics, fission and fusion, space flight . . . Let me at least put it to the council for a vote.

ADAMA: I cannot stop you from seeking the approval of the council, but you will not achieve it. They will not overrule Doctor Zee. He has never been wrong.

XAVIAR: The situation has never been this critical. And while he may be a mental mutant, he is still a beardless child! This has unbalanced him!

ADAMA: Well, let us say that the situation has unbalanced *someone*.

XAVIAR: Side with me, Adama. I could be a great leader. I can deliver us a planet capable of saving us now . . . not at some nebulous date centuries hence.

ADAMA: The concept is appealing. I must admit that. But I cannot vote against Doctor Zee.

XAVIAR: He's a freak! We're men! If you side with me, the council will listen.

ADAMA: I can't. Just consider the implications of introducing so much as a single change in the past. Kill a single man or woman who would otherwise have lived, and you will simultaneously be killing millions of their descendants.

XAVIAR: You and your Snowball Effect! How do we know it really works like that? Maybe history isn't really changed; maybe it all comes out the very same. Take the chance of birth: whether your parents decide to journey from one place to another or not only dictates the environment in which you are born. The fact remains that you are indeed born, you live, and you die.

ADAMA: And think of all the lives that would have been saved had, for example, Baltar had been raised in a different environment. Or take my own grandson, Boxey—excuse me, Troy. Had we not found him and his mother, he would not have saved the *Galactica* from the last Cylon attack, and then you would not be sitting here arguing with me. And yet he would have been born, he would have lived, and someday he will die.

XAVIAR: Even if you're right—and I'm not saying it for a second—you've still got a value judgment to make. If things remain as they are, the Cylons will sooner or later become aware of Earth's existence and totally destroy the planet and its entire population. However, if I were to introduce the marvels of science to primitive Earth, even at the cost of Earth's given history, at least they will have a chance for survival. They may not be the same men who live now, but at least they'll be human beings, men like us, and we'll be helping them to survive.

ADAMA: I don't deny that you're making very persuasive arguments. We have probably brought the Cylons too close. Earth stands in imminent risk of detection. But yet . . .

XAVIAR: But yet you won't oppose a mutant child who is a man only by the broadest of definitions. Is that it?

ADAMA: When all is said and done, that's it: I cannot oppose a man who has never been wrong.

XAVIAR: Well, I'm putting my case before the council. Recall Troy and Dillon and the others.

ADAMA: That would entail breaking radio silence.

XAVIAR: Don't give me that, Adama. We have half a hundred channels that are beyond the perception of any instruments the Earthmen have. It's beneath you to stall this way.

ADAMA: You insist on a vote of the council?

XAVIAR: It is my right.

ADAMA: Then I will recall my grandson.

10

The phone rang, and Sergeant Michael Lalor reached across his desk and picked it up.

"Lalor here . . . Yes, we've got them in the holding tank . . . Doctor *who?* . . . Well, just tell him there's no bail on these two . . . Don't worry, we'll keep tabs on them."

He hung up the phone and walked over to the cell where Troy and Dillon had been thrown in with a chronic alcoholic named Jimmy the Lush, who had taken up permanent weekend residence at the jail.

"Well, gentlemen," said Lalor, "it seems like some big shots are getting interested in you. Doctor Mortinson even tried to make bail for you, but it's no dice till we get a line on who you really are."

He walked back to his desk.

"What are big shots?" Troy mused.

"I don't know," answered his companion. "I don't even know what making bail is, but I suspect it's a legal maneuver to let us out of jail and the police aren't allowing it until they identify us."

"I hope that's not the case," said Troy. "Our invisibility fields won't protect the Vipers or the bikes more than another couple of hours, and the one I've got around our weapons and computers will be giving way

57

any minute now." He patted an invisible package on his
belt meaningfully.

"Hey," said Jimmy the Lush, who was sitting on the
floor in the corner of the cell, "either of you two guys
got a stogie?"

"A what?" asked Dillon.

"A stogie, a cigar," mumbled Jimmy. "Or maybe a
little Dago Red. I'm partial to Dago Red."

"He's partial to anything that pours," said Lalor,
who had heard Jimmy's last remark.

"I'm sorry," said Troy, "but we don't have any
liquid refreshment or stimulant with us."

"Oh, that's pretty, the way you talk," said Jimmy,
enthused. "I love the sound of the language."

"Especially your own," yelled Lalor from across the
room.

"Make fun of an old man if you want, but I used to
have a collection of poetry that would make your head
spin," said Jimmy. "Frost, Yeats, Whitman, Benet, I
knew all of them by heart."

"Sure you did, pal," laughed Lalor. "Where's your
collection now?"

"Sold it," said Jimmy.

"Why?"

"Anaconda Copper," said Jimmy. "Bought it on
margin at 80, and they made a margin call at 12½. I lost
everything."

"Sounds convincing," laughed Lalor. "Except that
Anaconda went through the floor in 1929, and you were
born in 1930."

"Well, *somebody* went broke on Anaconda," said
Jimmy.

"Yeah, poet, but it wasn't you," said Lalor.

"But it might have been," said Jimmy, cackling.
"You got to admit it makes a good story. Actually, I
blew it all on the Giants in the 1951 pennant race."

"They won in 1951," said Lalor. "Bobby Thomp-
son's home run."

"No respect," said Jimmy to Troy and Dillon. "No
sympathy. Actually, I didn't never blow my wad at all.

I've still got millions of dollars hid away.''

"That's nice,'' said Troy distractedly.

"And it's all yours if you can get me just a little sip of *vino*.''

"This guy's so far out of his mind that he probably won't notice if we turn our personal light deflection fields on,'' whispered Troy.

"Yeah,'' said Dillon. "But what about the police officer?''

"Sooner or later he's got to leave the room,'' said Troy. "We'll do it then. Even if our friend Jimmy here tells them what happened, no one will believe him.''

Dillon nodded. They ignored Jimmy as best they could, and a few moments later, when Sergeant Lalor was called away from his desk, they activated their invisibility screens.

"What the hell is going on here!'' screamed Lalor when he re-entered the room a minute later. "Where did those guys go?''

"Maybe it was the Packers,'' said Jimmy to no one in particular. "I lost my bundle betting on the Packers in the first Super Bowl.''

Lalor flung open the door to the cell, stepped inside as if to make sure his eyes weren't playing tricks on him, then slammed it shut behind him—and behind Troy and Dillon as well.

"But if I still had my millions,'' said Jimmy, "I'd bet every last penny of them that those two guys never left my cell.''

11

"Now, this mike will pick up everything you and the Doctor discuss about his connection with the terrorists," said Anderson, pinning a tiny microphone under Jamie's collar. "We'll be holding you on a long lens from the back of the truck. Try to get him to face this way as much as possible."

"I'll do my best, Mr. Anderson," said Jamie, looking at the police station about a block away.

"I know you will," said Anderson. "Now get going."

She had walked half the intervening distance when she heard a mildly familiar voice coming from out of the shadows to her left. "Don't do it, Jamie. He's a good man."

She took a step toward the voice, and Troy and Dillon seemed magically to appear before her. She blinked once, wrote it off to the tricks played by the shadows, then remembered who they were.

"What are you two doing out of jail?" she demanded.

"We felt that staying in jail was counterproductive," replied Dillon with the hint of a smile on his lips.

"Who the hell are those two bozos?" said Anderson, back in the truck. "Where did they come from?"

60

"I don't know," admitted his cameraman. "But I'm getting a good signal."

"Save your film," said Anderson. "They can't be all that important. It's Mortinson I want."

Jamie and the two warriors kept walking slowly toward the jail, speaking heatedly.

"You've got to get these journalists away from here while we talk to Doctor Mortinson," insisted Troy.

"I can't," said Jamie. "I just got this job, and I'm not going to blow it for a couple of kooks. How did you get out of jail?"

"We escaped," said Troy.

"You mean I've got a couple of escaped jailbirds right on camera?"

"No you don't," said Dillon, checking his wrist computer. "There's no power emanating from the camera."

She turned and signalled Anderson to turn the camera on. He shook his head and pointed to a man who was walking back and forth in front of the station.

Jamie sighed and followed the direction of his gesture. "It's him!" she exclaimed.

"Doctor Mortinson!" called Dillon.

Mortinson turned toward them and began approaching hesitantly.

"Miss Hamilton?" he said.

"Right," said Jamie.

"I expected you to come alone," said Mortinson, eyeing Troy and Dillon dubiously.

"These are the two gentlemen you wanted to talk about," Jamie informed him.

"But I thought . . . but of course," he said, staring at them. "Walls do not a prison make. Especially for someone like you." He extended his hand, and first Troy and then Dillon shook it.

"I seem to be a welcoming committee of one," continued Mortinson. "But if I am correct in my assumptions, and I almost have to be, there is no one on the face of this planet who could have done what you did at my computer today. Imagine inverting Aronson's

Lemma and combining it with Eisenstein's Irreducibility
Criterion to accelerate the half-life of uranium isotopes!
There was nothing in the entire body of work on the
subject that could have led to such a conclusion . . . but
of course, it's the only way to get to the proper pre-
liminary equations. No one on Earth could have come
up with it.''

A block away Anderson prodded his audio technician. ''What are they talking about?'' he demanded.

''Walls, prisons, computers . . . nothing that makes
any sense,'' came the answer.

''What's the matter with that girl?'' demanded
Anderson of no one in particular. ''Why doesn't she
dump those two guys and get on with the interview?''

And, one hundred yards away, Troy turned suddenly
to Mortinson. ''I suggest that we find another place to
talk. We're being observed.''

''You bet your boots you are,'' said Jamie. ''And I'm
not letting you guys out of my sight.''

''My car isn't far,'' said Mortinson, ignoring her. He
headed off for it, followed closely by Troy and Dillon.

''Hold everything!'' said Jamie, running after them.

She reached them just as they had climbed into the
sporty little roadster. Troy was seated in the back, and
was about to close the door when Jamie flung herself
into the automobile.

''Miss Hamilton,'' said Mortinson coldly, ''I appreciate all you've done for me, but I think we can get
along without you now.''

''Maybe you can, but I can't get along without you
three,'' said Jamie emphatically. ''There's no way I'm
getting out of here before you do.''

''We'd better take her along,'' said Troy. ''Time is
important.''

''As you wish,'' said Mortinson, starting the ignition.

The car raced off into the night, and Anderson
instructed his driver to follow it. Mortinson began picking his way through traffic, but couldn't shake Anderson's vehicle.

"Faster!" said Troy. "We've got to get beyond the sending range of Jamie's communication device!"

"What device?" demanded Jamie.

"The one you've got beneath your collar," said Troy. "We've known about it from the instant we met you tonight."

Mortinson stepped on the gas and still couldn't shake his pursuer.

Suddenly Dillon leaned over and edged himself into the driver's seat, almost colliding with a bus as he did so. "Excuse me, Doctor," he said, "but I'm a little more used to high speeds than you are."

Mortinson merely swallowed and nodded his head.

Dillon pressed the accelerator to the floor and pealed around a corner on two wheels as the sound of screeching rubber permeated the cool California night. Within seconds he had two police cars on his tail as well as the news truck.

"Dillon, you've never driven one of these things before!" yelled Troy, his hand clutching an armrest. "Are you sure you know what you're doing?"

"I've been watching him," replied Dillon with more confidence than he felt. "It looks easy."

"What do you mean, you've never driven a car before?" screamed Jamie as the speedometer topped 110 miles per hour and Dillon hit another turn.

"I wouldn't think," said Mortinson through clenched teeth, his eyes tightly shut, "that these men had cars where they come from."

"Where don't they have cars?" demanded Jamie.

Further conversation was interrupted by the sudden beeping of Troy's communicator.

"Troy here," he said, withdrawing it from his belt and speaking into it.

"This is Adama . . . you are to return to the Galactica *at once."*

"Who is he talking to?" asked Jamie. "His service?"

"I hesitate to ask," replied Mortinson.

"On our way," said Troy.

"Galactica *out*."

"What's a *Galactica*?" asked Jamie as Troy put his communicator away.

"Doctor," said Troy, ignoring Jamie's question, "if I can ask you to keep what little we've discussed in confidence, we'll have to arrange to get together again as soon as possible."

"But the formula you left in my lab . . ." protested Mortinson. "It's incomplete! I must have the rest! It's the answer to our problems. You've seen the riots . . ."

"Consider it a token of our good faith," said Troy. "If you keep your silence, what we've given you is just the beginning. We'll give you the rest when we return."

"But when will that be?" said Mortinson.

"It makes no difference, Doctor," said Jamie. "*You* may be willing to work on faith, but *I'm* staying with these two guys to the end of the line."

"That's quite impossible," said Troy firmly.

"You try to lose me and I'll blab everything I know," said Jamie with equal firmness.

"Troy?" said Dillon. "Our first mandate was to remain incognito . . ."

"Well," said Jamie, looking at the ever-increasing trail of police cars, "you're sure doing a hell of a job!"

12

COMMANDER ADAMA: What's happened?
What's gone wrong?

DOCTOR ZEE: A miscalculation.

COMMANDER ADAMA: I thought it was impossible for you to miscalculate anything.

DOCTOR ZEE: This is not *my* miscalculation. It is yours. Why did you not tell me that Xaviar wanted to use my Time Warp Synthesizer?

COMMANDER ADAMA: What has happened?

DOCTOR ZEE: Rather than wait for the vote of the council, he has left us, Adama . . . for someplace, or rather some time, in Earth's past.

COMMANDER ADAMA: That fool . . . that utter fool! I never thought he'd do it on his own!

DOCTOR ZEE: What is his plan?

COMMANDER ADAMA: To change Earth's present technonological development, to accelerate it by altering the past, if that's possible.

DOCTOR ZEE: Oh, it's quite possible. But it's also deadly.

COMMANDER ADAMA: That maniac! We must bring him back!

DOCTOR ZEE: A chase through thousands of years of history: *that* should be interesting.

COMMANDER ADAMA: Is it possible to know into

what era, or preferably to what date, he has escaped?

DOCTOR ZEE: Yes, I will be able to tell you that after some computations. But I cannot prevent him from moving on.

COMMANDER ADAMA: If we keep him constantly on the move through Time, can we keep him from unleashing his madness?

DOCTOR ZEE: Possibly. But remember—in your pursuit of him, you can do as much damage as Xaviar. You must be very, very careful, Adama . . . or that planet below us could disappear in the twinkling of an eye, even as we look at it.

13

"I don't imagine this thing flies, does it?" asked Dillon as the police cars made up some of the ground they had lost on the last corner.

"No," said Mortinson. "It's powered by a very simple internal combustion engine, which burns gasoline, which in turn drives the pistons, which turn a simple drive shaft."

"But it doesn't fly?" persisted Dillon.

"No," said Mortinson. "It doesn't fly."

"We've got to elude these people, Dillon," said Troy. "Our invisibility fields are past due for recharging. If anyone stumbles across those ships now . . ."

"Ships?" said Jamie. "What ships?"

Troy's communicator beeped again.

"Boxey, this is Adama. Get up here quick! Crisis situation!"

"We're encountering a few problems," replied Troy. "We'll get there as soon as we can."

"Make sure you do . . . Adama out."

"What do you suppose is going on up there?" asked Dillon.

"It's got to be the Cylons," said Troy. "What else could cause a crisis situation?"

"It may be none of my business," said Mortinson. "But what's a Cylon?"

67

"You're absolutely right, sir," said Troy.

"What?"

"It *is* none of your business. And if we can get out of this situation quickly, we'll do our best to see that it never becomes your business."

"I'm afraid I don't understand," said Mortinson.

"Believe me," said Troy. "You're much better off this way. Dillon, I don't care what you do, but do *something*!"

Dillon hit a ninety-degree turn at midblock, slammed on the brakes, and went through a furniture store window. The car skidded some two hundred feet through the display room before crunching to a halt.

Even before it was totally at rest, Troy and Dillon had thrown open the car's door and leaped out.

"We'll replace your vehicle when we return, sir," said Dillon.

"Think nothing of it," said Mortinson, counting his arms and legs and coming up with the proper number, much to his amazement. "What you gave me is worth infinitely more."

"Good-bye, sir," said Troy. "We've got to get out of here before the police arrive."

"Not without me," said Jamie.

"There's no time to argue!" said Dillon, and Troy nodded. He gestured Jamie to follow him and raced out through a fire exit.

"Will you be all right, sir?" called Dillon.

"I'll be fine," Mortinson assured him. "And I'll be quiet."

Dillon flashed him a smile, then raced out into the night to join Troy and Jamie. When he got there two policemen could be heard walking around the side of the building, and the two warriors switched on their invisibility screens, posturing Jamie so that she was included in the field. The two policemen walked past, missing them by perhaps eighteen inches. After they rounded the building and passed from sight, Troy and Dillon switched off the fields.

"Okay, I give up," said Jamie. "How did you do that?"

"We haven't time to explain," said Troy, walking to a parked police car. "And this time I'm driving the machine."

"If I tell you guys something you need to know, will you take me with you?" said Jamie.

"We can't," said Troy.

"Then you're going to wind up back in jail in five minutes."

Troy looked up at the sky. The *Galactica* was up there somewhere, and Adama was in trouble. "All right," he said quickly. "You've got a deal."

"Okay. Don't swipe a police car. They've got their own private radio band, and you won't get half a mile before every cop in the city knows where you are."

"We'll just turn the radio off," said Dillon.

"It won't matter," said Jamie. "They'll report the theft in less than a minute, and every cop in town will start relaying your co-ordinates to every other cop. They'll hem you in so fast it'll make your head spin."

"So what do you suggest?" said Troy.

"If you've *got* to steal a car, at least steal a private one," said Jamie.

"Makes sense," said Dillon.

Troy nodded. "There are a batch parked on the next block. Which one do you suggest?"

"Easy," said Jamie. "Whichever one has keys in it."

"Why keys?" asked Troy.

"Because I don't know how to hot-wire a car, and you two don't even know how to drive."

"Hot-wire?" repeated Troy.

"Start the ignition without keys," explained Jamie.

"No problem," said Troy. "Which of these vehicles looks like the best to you?"

"The blue '79 Continental," said Jamie, indicating a huge, chrome-covered car.

"Then that's the one we'll borrow," said Troy. He walked over, opened the unlocked door, and slid in behind the steering wheel. Then, unfastening his sensor, he aimed it at the engine, instructed it to activate the motor, and a moment later the car was humming and throbbing with power.

"Spies, right?" said Jamie, sliding into the back seat with Dillon. "I mean, nobody except James Bond types have the kind of equipment you guys carry. But which side are you on? Are you working for us, or is Doctor Mortinson a commie?"

"What's a commie?" asked Dillon pleasantly as Troy raced through the night, checking directions on his wrist computer from time to time. Jamie finally gave up asking questions, and they rode in silence to the gas station near which they had left their bikes.

They left the Continental by a gas pump and walked to a small knoll half a mile distant. The bikes were plainly visible.

"Oh-oh!" said Dillon. "Troy, if the energizer on the bikes' invisibility field has run down, and we switched it on *after* we left the Vipers . . ."

"Then the ships are probably visible!" said Troy, completing the sentence. "We haven't got any time to waste!"

They turned on their turbo thrusters and a moment later the two men, with Jamie clinging desperately to Troy, were racing at very near the speed of sound to the spot where they had left their Vipers.

"Damn!" said Troy as they came to a halt almost a mile away.

"They're visible," said Dillon.

"And they've got a bunch of soldiers standing guard over them," added Troy.

"What are those things?" said Jamie, who was just recovering from her wild ride. "I've seen Phantom jets close up, but they didn't look anything like this."

"Be quiet, Jamie," said Troy. "I've got to think."

"What are you talking about?" said Jamie. "You've come into my life, and made me an accessory to a jailbreak and a car theft, and taken me for a zillion-mile-an-hour ride, and messed me up with my boss, and almost got me killed in a car wreck. And now the cops are after me, and for all I know you're Russian spies, and you're telling me to be quiet? If I had half a brain, I'd be screaming for help right now!"

"Not now," said Troy.

"Don't you 'Not now' me, Mister!" snapped Jamie. "I want to know who you are and what you are going to do about this mess you've gotten me into."

Suddenly a police siren shattered the night air.

"My God, they've been following us!" said Jamie. "It took them a little longer to get here, but we sure weren't hard to track down."

"Troy, we've got to do something," said Dillon.

"I'm open to suggestions," responded Troy.

Then Jamie jumped to her feet and ran about twenty yards in the direction of the ships.

"Jamie, get down!" whispered Dillon.

"You two have turned me into a fugitive, and I'm not going to take this rap alone. Either you explain what you're up to to the cops and the army, or you agree to take me with you so I can get the whole story. You've got five seconds to make up your minds, and then I start screaming."

"All right!" whispered Troy. "You win!"

"You agree with him?" she asked Dillon.

Dillon nodded, and with a smile of triumph she rejoined them.

"We'll have to use the invisibility screens again," said Troy. "I don't see how we can take the bikes with us, though."

"Should we destroy them?" asked Dillon.

"Ordinarily I'd say yes," answered Troy, "but if we do anything to attract attention they might put guards in the Vipers. We don't want to have to hurt anyone."

"That's a laugh!" said Jamie.

"Believe it or not, Jamie, we're here to help you," said Troy.

"Not," said Jamie emphatically.

They activated the screens and walked, undetected, to the ships. Troy took Jamie's hand and boosted her into his Viper, whispering, "Hang on and keep your eyes closed."

"Why?"

"Just once try believing me," he whispered back, swinging into the pilot's seat.

"Ready?" came Dillon's whisper over Troy's radio.

"Ready," said Troy.

"Maybe," said Jamie as the acceleration threw her against the back of her seat, "this wasn't such a good idea!" She had begun her sentence on the ground; she finished it at a height of four thousand miles and climbing.

"I think I can say with certainty," remarked Dillon as they approached the *Galactica* a few minutes later, "that our first attempt at contact was not quite the smashing success that I had anticipated."

Jamie, who was too terrified to speak, nodded her head vigorously.

14

MORTINSON UNHARMED

(UPI) Doctor Alfred Mortinson, Nobel Prize laureate, was rescued by Los Angeles police this evening after being kidnapped by two criminals who had earlier been arrested in the vicinity of his office at the Pacific Institute of Technology.

Mortinson was unharmed though shaken by his ordeal, and refused all comment.

Police speculate that his abductors belong to an antinuclear fringe group from the northern part of the state who may have intended holding Mortinson captive until local governments agreed to abandon all nuclear research and close all nuclear power plants.

The two men are still at large and are believed to be holding television reporter Jamie Hamilton as a hostage. Detectives are scrutinizing film footage taken by award-winning journalist Dana Anderson from a mobile news unit, but as yet the identities of the kidnappers remain unknown.

15

FOR IMMEDIATE RELEASE:

(Science News Service) For the second time in less than 24 hours, the Los Angeles area was flooded with reports of UFO sightings.

According to Professor Stuart Brownstein of the UCLA Department of Astronomy, the usual causes of such sightings—meteorites, low-flying civilian aircraft, and various atmospheric disturbances—do not explain these particular sightings, most of which had a pair of objects flying almost straight *upward* at enormous speeds.

"Almost ninety percent of the sightings agree that these objects were moving perpendicular both to the Earth and to any tangential planes," said Professor Brownstein. "And I think there have been too many reported sightings to assume all these people were just looking at swamp gas, or whatever the Air Force is pushing these days."

Professor Brownstein declined to speculate on the causes of the sightings.

16

FROM THE RECOLLECTIONS OF
COMMANDER ADAMA AND DOCTOR ZEE:

Boomer did a double take when he saw the respiratory readout on Troy's Viper, then promptly signalled Adama.

"Yes?" said Adama.

"The last two Vipers are returning from Earth," Boomer reported. "But we've got a little problem."

"Of what nature?"

"There seem to be two people aboard Troy's Viper. The chromosome count confirms that the second entity is a human female."

"But that's strictly against orders!" thundered Adama.

"It's possible that they could be in some kind of trouble. After all, it's been quite some time since we sent out the recall message."

"We'll see," said Adama grimly. "Have them report to my chambers the moment they arrive."

"The female too?" asked Boomer.

"Yes," said Adama. "I don't imagine that we have anything further to hide from her."

The two Vipers executed smooth landings and an armed escort ushered Troy, Dillon and Jamie out of the landing bay and into the interior of the *Galactica*.

"It's as big as a city!" exclaimed Jamie as they made their way to Adama's quarters.

"It's far more than a city," said Troy. "It has had to serve as our planet."

"Then your last planet wasn't Earth?" said Jamie.

"No," said Troy. "We're not from Earth."

"But . . . but you look just like us!"

"The race of man is not unique to Earth," said Dillon.

"And your English . . . you speak it perfectly."

"Preparation for contact," said Troy. "We also speak Italian, Russian, French, Arabic, Chinese, Spanish and a number of lesser dialects. Right, Dillon?"

"Languages are a snap, *n'est-ce pas*?" grinned Dillon.

"And you're really not from Earth!" repeated Jamie. "I mean, even after we got into your spaceship I figured you were CIA or some super-NASA group." She looked around her and shook her head vigorously, as if this would make the walls of the *Galactica* recede, to be replaced by more familiar surroundings. "I wonder if this trip wasn't a major mistake."

"Our Commander is likely to feel much the same way about it," said Troy apprehensively as they reached Adama's door.

A guard pressed a button and the panel slid open. Adama stood with his back to them, his eyes on the viewscreen that presented him with a vision of fully half the galaxy. As Dillon coughed nervously he turned to face them.

"Well, Captain Troy and Lieutenant Dillon . . . and guest. I hope you realize the gravity in which you've placed this young lady, as well as ourselves."

"They didn't have any choice," Jamie spoke up. "I'm Jamie Hamilton of United Broadcasting. You're—?"

"Commander Adama."

Jamie whipped out a cassette recorder and held it out toward Adama, who flinched but held his ground, eyeing the machine warily.

"Would you mind repeating that?" she said.

"What is that?" Adama demanded.

"Probably some kind of recording device," said Dillon. "She's associated with Earth's communication media."

"I assume you had no choice other than to bring her back with you?" said Adama.

"I insisted," said Jamie smugly.

"That's true," Troy admitted. "And your recall order was battle urgent. It left us no time to find alternatives."

"Besides," added Dillon, "if we hadn't taken her along, she would have made public everything she had seen."

"And she saw a lot?" asked Adama, raising an eyebrow.

Dillon nodded vigorously.

"Well, young lady, we'll just have to deal with you as best we can," said Adama resignedly.

"I must warn you that abusing the press is dealt with very harshly where I come from," said Jamie.

Adama could not resist a smile at that. "I assure you that you'll be treated quite well for the duration of your stay here."

"Duration?" said Jamie. "That has an unpleasant ring of semi-permanance to it. I only came up here for a story."

"Unfortunately, your story is not one that we can permit you to publish for the foreseeable future," said Adama. He turned to Troy and Dillon. "We've got a problem. Our mission to Earth must be suspended."

"But why?" said Troy. "I think we were on the verge of making some real progress. We got to Doctor Mortinson."

"And?" said Adama.

"And if the rest of the scientific community is as receptive as he was," said Dillon, "I don't forsee any serious difficulties in gaining their confidence and acceptance."

"We'll have to take up the subject later," said Adama. "Right now we have an emergency to deal with."

"What could be more important than preparing the Earth to defend itself?" said Troy, puzzled.

"Defend itself?" said Jamie. "From who?"

Adama ignored her. "Xaviar has commandeered a ship and returned to the Earth in the year 1944 of the Christian era."

"Commander," said Troy, "if Earth isn't advanced enough to help us now, what can Xaviar possibly hope to accomplish back in 1944?"

"You mean you guys can travel through time?" exclaimed Jamie unbelievingly.

"You travel through space, don't you?" said Dillon. "Time's just another dimension."

"Getting back to Xaviar . . ." said Troy.

"Perhaps we'd better have a talk with Doctor Zee," suggested Adama, opening his door and leading the way to the fourteen-year-old genius's chambers.

"I repeat," said Troy: "What can Xaviar expect to accomplish in 1944?"

"He intends to accelerate Earth's technology by introducing superior weaponry into her past," said Adama patiently.

"But that's ridiculous!" said Troy.

"Not at all," said Adama. "The Snowball Effect clearly stipulates . . ."

"No, that's not what I mean," said Troy. "But why 1944? That only allows thirty-six years for development. Why not three thousand years ago? Or thirty thousand? Why not hunt up an ape sitting in a tree two million years ago and give him a bow and arrow?"

"An excellent question, Captain Troy," said Doctor Zee, speaking for the first time. "But the closer to the present you are when you attempt to adjust the past, the less powerful will be the Snowball Effect."

"Could you explain that, please?" said Troy.

"Certainly," said Doctor Zee. "If you introduce no change prior to 1944, no matter what happens the likelihood is that the major nations will still exist thirty-six years later. The air shouldn't be so polluted as to be unbreathable, the oceans shouldn't teem with radioactive waste, there should be no new major languages which our translator banks will have to master. Now let's take your hypothetical apeman of two million years ago. It's possible his species would grow into Man—but it's equally possible that they would destroy each other, turn Earth into a huge garbage dump teeming with radiation, or simply take a different turn on the evolutionary ladder and not become men at all.''

"I see," said Troy.

"It's a gamble from Xaviar's point of view," continued Doctor Zee. "He wants to go far enough back in time to make the necessary changes, but remain close enough to the present so that the changes don't snowball all out of proportion. It's like a man standing atop an icy mountain, pursued by a large carnivore. He knows he can defeat it even though he has nothing but a tiny snowball in his hand. He begins rolling the snowball down the mountain, and at a certain point the snowball will be large enough to dispatch the beast. But if the snowball continues to roll and accumulate more matter, eventually it will be too big for him to control or even lift.''

"But why 1944?" asked Dillon.

"Because the German rocketry experts were experimenting with the V-2," said Doctor Zee.

"But the Americans harnessed the atom in 1945!" said Jamie. "Why didn't he go there?"

"Because the Americans never used the atom for warfare after 1945," said Doctor Zee. "On the other hand, from what I have been able to glean from our inadequate supply of information concerning Earth's political history, Germany's Third Reich was a military machine that would have continued to perfect any weapons Xaviar placed into their hands.''

"And this Xaviar guy's really in Germany now?" said Jamie. "In 1944?"

"Correct," said Doctor Zee.

"Then he didn't pull it off!" said Jamie triumphantly. The others regarded her silently. "Don't you see? If he had accomplished his mission, I would come from a world in which Germany won the war. But it didn't, so he must have failed!"

"You know, it makes sense at that," admitted Dillon.

"A thing can make sense without being right," said Doctor Zee. "Dillon, both you and this young woman are making the mistake of viewing Time as a straight-line progression."

"Isn't it?" asked Dillon.

"Only up to a point," said Doctor Zee. "You see, there is only one past, but there are an infinite number of futures. Now, without the benefit of time travel, past and present merge in an immutable series of events, though any occurrence made in the present instant will have immense and unforeseen consequences in the future. And indeed, Dillon, were time travel impossible, I would agree with you that Germany lost the war and didn't develop any super weapons.

"But Xaviar has changed all that," continued the mental mutant. "*His* present is now 1944, and any action he takes there will have an effect, possibly a disastrous one, on the course of Earth's history."

"But it didn't happen!" repeated Jamie.

"Wrong, my dear," said Doctor Zee. "It merely hasn't happened yet. The fact that we are all here discussing the topic, and that you come from a world in which the Third Reich didn't develop the Ultimate Weapon, merely means that we haven't done anything wrong *yet*."

"I'm afraid you've lost me, Doctor Zee," said Adama.

"We must send Troy and Dillon into the past after Xaviar. It is their job to stop him from whatever he intends to do. If they succeed, all will be as it is; if not, then this young woman and her particular Earth will blink out of existence to be replaced by the one Xaviar has created. Neither she nor the Earth nor even this conversation will ever have been anything but an alternative future which, like an infinite number of other futures, did not come to pass."

"Then we're not actually in a hurry," said Troy. "I

mean, as long as all we have to do is stop Xaviar back in 1944, it doesn't make any difference whether we leave now or five years from now, as long as we appear at the right moment in 1944.''

"If we were free from all other considerations you would be quite correct," said Doctor Zee. "But that is not the case.''

"I don't understand," said Troy.

"We've got the Cylon forces to consider," said Doctor Zee. "To remain in the vicinity of Earth for five years, or even five days, would be to invite disaster to our fellow humans on the planet's surface. And to leave and then return when you felt you had assimilated enough of Earth's history would be to call even more attention to this sector of the galaxy. No, Troy, you must leave as soon as possible. And you must leave with the knowledge that should you fail, the *Galactica* you return to may not be the same one you left, and the Earth will most certainly not be the one you just visited.''

"I might be able to help," said Jamie hesitantly.

"In what way?" said Adama.

"I was a history major before I became a journalist," she said, gathering enthusiasm as she spoke. "I'm sure I can be useful to you—in exchange for exclusive rights to the story, plus film at six.''

"Film at six?" said Dillon.

"You wouldn't understand," said Jamie. "But that's my deal: let me go with Troy and Dillon and I'll help in every way I can.''

"It's out of the question," said Adama. "The situation is deadly enough without dragging a civilian into it.''

"On the contrary, Adama," interposed Doctor Zee. "Our knowledge of Earth's past is growing with every hour, but for the reasons I've stated, our two warriors do not have the luxury of remaining aboard the *Galactica* until we can thoroughly brief them on the history and customs of the era to which they must go. If this woman is truly a student of history . . .''

"Try me," said Jamie with more confidence than she felt.

"The time-distance co-ordinates would seem to place Xaviar in a small hamlet in the nation known as Germany, which at that time is being ruled by the Nazis. You have heard of them?"

"Who hasn't?" said Jamie. "They were responsible for the coining of the word 'genocide'."

"Genocide?" said Troy.

"The wholesale slaughter of human beings in enormous quantities," said Jamie. "The practice originated —and ended—in World War Two."

"World War *Two*?" said Adama unbelievingly.

"Yes," said Jamie. "To quote a comic strip character named Pogo Possum, I guess they had to have a second war to decide who won the first one."

"This is no time for levity," said Doctor Zee emotionlessly.

"All right," said Jamie. "Through a series of misjudgments and accidents that would have been funny had the results not been so grim, Europe stumbled into a multi-national war in 1914. The major powers were Germany on the one side, and England and France on the other. The United States entered on the side of England and France after a couple of years, and Germany surrendered in 1918. But the terms that the allies forced upon Germany were so untenable that her economy collapsed, her government couldn't function, and numerous other situations all came together to form a climate whereby a madman named Adolph Hitler, who had been a mere corporal in World War One, could take control of the German government in the early 1930s."

"By force?" asked Adama.

"The force came later," said Jamie. "The wild part of it all is that Hitler was voted into office. He promised to give the downtrodden German nation back its self-respect."

"Reasonable on the surface of it," said Adama.

"Ah, but there are all kinds of ways of accomplishing

it," said Jamie. "First of all, he gave the Germans a scapegoat: the Jews."

"Who were they?" asked Troy.

"They were, and are, a people who practice the religion which gave birth to Christianity," said Jamie. "When Hitler came to power there were perhaps twelve million Jews in the world. When the dust had settled he had killed more than half of them. He had most of them shipped to concentration camps, where they were slaughtered in gas chambers and buried in mass graves. Some, a few hundred thousand at least, were turned into soap, and a few even had their skins made into lampshades. It was hideous. And at the same time he was making his followers feel superior—indeed, they finally accepted his notion that they were a Master Race—he was building up a huge war machine, which got the economy back on its feet. The war began innocuously; he marched into a neighboring country, claiming that he needed more living space for his people and stating that this was nothing but a border dispute between two nations. The wild part is that everyone, or almost everyone, believed him, despite the fact that he had outlined his plans for world conquest in a book called *Mein Kampf*. Sometimes I think no one except Winston Churchill ever read that book before 1939!

"At any rate, Germany began conquering the European nations one by one. Most took only a day or two before they fell. France had its Maginot Line, a miles-long line of defense that they felt was invulnerable. Hitler simply marched around it, and France fell within a week. But when he went up against Russia and England, they fought him to a standstill. By 1942 the United States had declared war on Germany, Italy and Japan—though Japan was a separate case, and was Hitler's ally only insofar as both were at war with the United States—and in 1943 we shipped troops into Africa and Italy. By 1944 the handwriting was on the wall. Germany finally fell in 1945, and was divided by the four great powers—Russia, the United States,

England, and France (though I'm sure I don't know what ever qualified France as a great 20th Century power)—and it remains divided to this day."

"You see, Adama," said Doctor Zee. "She *can* be of help. We don't even know what a Swastika, the Nazi symbol, looks like. I think it is imperative that she accompany our two warriors into Germany's past."

"You are right, as always," said Adama with a sigh.

"Some country we're going to," said Troy. "Didn't any of the Germans stand up to him?"

"It wasn't as easy to stand up to the Gestapo as you might think," said Jamie. "There was an underground, to be sure, just as there were undergrounds in all the nations Hitler conquered—but they were never as big nor as active as modern fiction writers would have people believe. Don't forget: not much misses the eyes and ears of a police state that's more than a decade old."

"True," agreed Doctor Zee. "Which makes it all the more imperative that you accompany Troy and Dillon and help them avoid exposing their lack of knowledge of the time and the area."

"All right," said Adama. "Get her outfitted and be prepared to take off immediately thereafter."

"Yes, sir," said Troy. He and Dillon escorted Jamie from Doctor Zee's chambers and left the youthful genius deep in conversation with Adama.

"How, exactly, do we get to the past?" said Jamie as they began gathering her gear.

"According to Doctor Zee," began Troy, "time travel is possible only after we've exceeded the speed of light and . . ."

"Wait a minute!" said Jamie. "Nothing can exceed the speed of light. Einstein's theory states that when your speed approaches that of light, your mass approaches infinity, which means that to reach the speed of light you'd have to have an infinite mass, and that means that not all the energy in the Universe could power it, and . . ." Her voice trailed off and she scratched her head. "But you're here, and you *had* to travel at light speeds to get here, didn't you?"

Troy nodded.

"Well," shrugged Jamie. "Einstein also said that his theory might only be a local phenomenon. And Jamie Hamilton says, never spit in the eye of a fact."

"Actually," said Troy, "we achieve faster-than-light speeds by using a drive based on the tachyon, which is a faster-than-light subatomic particle. I don't understand how it works, but I do know how to pilot a ship. I'll leave the theorizing to Doctor Zee."

"So, back to time travel," said Jamie. "How does it work?"

"Well, as I understand it, merely traveling at faster-than-light speeds isn't enough to go back in Time; all it does is get you from one point to another very fast. But there is a time-warp factor dealing with stellar rotation that cropped up in Doctor Zee's equations, and he's programmed our Vipers' computers to travel back to exactly the moment he wants, which is sometime in 1944."

"And our computers are so sensitive," continued Dillon, "that we'll reappear in normal space-time over Germany. Not bad for a fourteen-year-old kid, eh?"

"Who is he?" asked Jamie. "Or maybe I should ask, *what* is he?"

"Hopefully he's the salvation of the human race," said Troy, carrying Jamie's gear to his Viper. "He's millions, billions of years ahead of his time on a cerebral scale. He was born in space, aboard the *Galactica*; without him we'd never have survived to find Earth."

"I get the very strong impression," said Jamie, "that everything we've discussed is just an appetizer, a prelude, and that your real problems have nothing to do with Earth."

"Right now," said Troy, boosting her into the Viper and then swinging his own lithe body into the pilot's seat, "our only concern is Earth. We can't solve one problem without solving the other." He turned on his radio. "Ready, Dillon?"

"Ready," came the answer from Dillon's Viper.

He turned back to Jamie. "You might be interested in keeping your eye on the scanner. You'll catch glimpses along our journey as the computer samples the co-ordinates to make sure we're on track. And now," he added, pressing the Viper's accelerator, "say good-bye to 1980."

She did so—but it was 1944 by the time the words were formed.

Part 2:

THEN

17

Jamie opened her eyes.

"Good morning," smiled Troy from his seat at the Viper control panel. "You passed out. Welcome to June 4, 1944."

"What happened?" she asked.

"I can't give you all the scientific gobbledegook," said Troy, "but when we travel through Time we move out of normal space-time, into a Universe—or rather a passage through a Universe—of non-causality."

"Non-causality?" repeated Jamie.

Troy nodded. "No cause and effect. Patternless lights, events that have no rhyme or reason, noises without a source. Your mind couldn't accept the testimony of your senses, and did the only thing it was capable of to preserve its notion of the way things are supposed to be: it passed out, went to sleep, shut down for a while in the face of a batch of data that bore no resemblance to anything familiar or logical."

"You stayed awake?" she asked.

"No need to feel ashamed, Jamie," said Dillon over the radio. "Troy and I have been conditioned for it. Believe me, the first time Doctor Zee simulated the effect of time travel, it took them three hours to wake me up!"

"Where are we now?" Jamie wanted to know.

89

"About thirty thousand feet above a little Bavarian village," said Troy. "It looks innocuous from up here, but I gather it's where they've got the prototypes of their more advanced V-2 rockets."

"And if you want to know *when* we are," said Dillon unhappily, "we're three weeks later than we should be."

"How could that happen?" asked Troy.

"I don't know," said Dillon, "except that time travel is pretty new even to Doctor Zee. Missing our mark by three weeks over a period of thirty-six years isn't so bad. I just wish if we had to be wrong, we could have arrived early."

"How do you know you're late?" asked Jamie.

"Our Vipers' computers were locked onto the electron discharge from Xaviar's ship," said Troy. "I guess even the computers must have been confused during the non-causal part of our journey."

"Well," said Dillon, "what do we do—go back and try again?"

"I don't think so," said Troy. "First of all, there's no guarantee we could get any closer to the right moment next time around. And second, whatever Xaviar's got in mind, it's going to take him a while to work his way up the power structure's ladder."

"Couldn't he just deposit some weapons and leave?" asked Jamie.

"No," said Troy. "Our weapons are pretty complex. Even if the Germans figured out how to use them, they'd need Xaviar to teach them the principles and show them how to build more."

"You're not giving the Germans much credit for brainpower," said Jamie. "They've produced some of the greatest scientists in our history."

"True," said Troy, "but they all operate on certain principles delineated by Isaac Newton and your Doctor Einstein—and our weapons aren't based on those principles. From what little I read of your history, a philosopher named Aristotle once declared that everything in the world was composed of four elements—

earth, air, fire and water—and it was more than fifteen hundred years before anyone questioned that statement. No, Xaviar has got to make sure he's in a position to show them what to do with our weapons, to guide them in making more. That's probably why he's chosen the V-2 rocket to start with; since it's a prototype, all he has to do is improve its expected performance and he'll probably be given the budget and the authority to do 'research' on an even better weapon system, which is doubtless just what he wants.''

"And he has a three-week head start on us?" said Jamie gloomily.

"It may not be all that difficult to hunt him down," said Troy. "After all, Dillon and I have had some firsthand experience concerning the difficulty of trying to appear inconspicuous in an alien society—and Xaviar's not trying to lose himself in a crowd. He's got to impress the German leaders with his abilities. If he makes a mistake they're going to try to arrest him, and he'll be forced to reveal himself if he uses any of our weapons or our invisibility field to remain free. Also, we know his target, so we're not going to waste a lot of time looking for him in farm fields or among the members of the underground.''

"What's to stop us from giving ourselves away in the process?" asked Jamie.

"Well, we're rather hoping that *you* will stop us," smiled Troy. "By the way, how's your German?"

"Passable," said Jamie. "I had three years of it in high school and two in college. But I'm sure I've got a heavy American accent, and that's got to stand out like a sore thumb in wartime."

"Then let us do the talking whenever possible," said Troy.

"Where did you learn German?"

"The same place we learned English," said Dillon over the radio.

"Right," said Troy. "Ten minutes with Doctor Zee's Language Educator and you can speak almost any tongue in the galaxy like a native. If we gave ourselves away at various times on Earth, it was our lack of knowledge of certain customs or portions of your technology, not our accents.''

"True," said Jamie. "But follow my lead when we start interacting with the Germans. You may speak the language a little better, but you're going to be babes in the woods when it comes to knowing what you're talking about."

"Agreed," said Troy.

"I hate to interrupt," said Dillon, "but six German aircraft just took off from the airfield where they're keeping the V-2."

Jamie looked down. "I can't tell from here if they're Forkkers or Messerschmidts."

"What's the difference?" asked Troy.

"None, really, considering what we're flying. Let's blow those filthy Nazis out of the sky!"

"We can't do that, Jamie," said Dillon.

"Why not?"

"Our mission is to apprehend Xaviar, not to help him change the past. If we kill one of these guys, and he otherwise would have survived the war and had three kids, and each of them had grown up to have a couple of children, and . . ."

"I know," sighed Jamie. "The old rice problem."

"Rice problem?" said Troy. "What's that?"

"It's an old story about a Chinese peasant who did a service for his ruler. The ruler offered him anything he wanted in the kingdom, and the peasant said that he would like someone to produce a chessboard. This was done—it's a game requiring sixty-four squares—and he said that his wish was for a single grain of rice on the first square, two on the second, four on the third, eight on the fourth, and so on. The ruler consented, and the peasant owned all the rice in the world before half the squares were used up."

"A simple geometrical progression," agreed Troy. "And it's the same thing when you go into the past and kill someone."

"I hate to break into a charming and fascinating conversation," said Dillon, "but the German aircraft will overtake us in about half a minute."

"What are those small projectiles that they're firing?" asked Troy.

"Bullets!" exclaimed Jamie. "Let's get out of here!"

"Good advice," grunted Troy, pulling the nose of his Viper up and firing his turbos. Dillon did likewise, and an instant later they had vanished from the skies.

"*Dumkoffs!*" said the German ground control radio. "The Americans have no airplanes capable of such speeds. You almost shot our own rockets out of the sky!"

"But they bore no German insignia," said one of the pilots.

"What else could they have been?" snapped the officer on the ground. "Bring your planes back to base and don't mention this to anyone—or we're all going to be seeing duty at the Russian front!"

A word to the wise was more than sufficient.

18

I took off from a small field in the South of France, no thanks to Charles de Gaulle, who had thrown so much red tape in our way that the project almost didn't get off the ground. I sure don't know why the French worship a muttonhead like that; I guess all the better generals and more rational men have been killed in the war.

I was flying a small Mosquito bomber with English insignia, which also didn't make much sense to me. I know it's a joint British-American venture, but hell, the Germans will shoot an English plane down just as quick as one of ours. Oh, well, I'm just the muscle; the brainpower must have its reasons.

Anyway, I used what cloud cover I could find, but it vanished when I got within about 300 air miles of Obersalzberg, Hilter's sometime-retreat that was my destination. The Fuehrer was in Berlin, but he wasn't what I was after, anyway; I think the bigwigs in Washington and London had an idea that his own generals were on the brink of murdering him for us. But Obersalzberg was also where they were working on the much-publicized but not-yet-seen V-2 rockets. And the V-2 (or V-2s, if there were more than a single prototype) was my target.

After the sky cleared, I went into a quick power dive

94

and leveled off at about 200 feet. I knew the British radar couldn't pick up anything that low-flying, and while we assumed the Germans hadn't developed radar yet, the odds were that even if they had it, flying this low would keep me unobserved.

It worked, too—until I was within about six miles of Obersalzberg. Then a pair of Messerschmidts started zeroing in on me. They came from such a height that I suspect they were returning home after chasing some other Allied ship out of their sky, but where they came from wasn't as important as how good they were. And they were plenty good.

I banked to the left and started climbing, but I couldn't shake them. Then I figured I'd show them some old county fair flying that I used to earn meal money with, and see what they were really made of.

I pulled back on the controls, gunned the engine, and flew straight up at a 90-degree angle with the ground. I remembered to scream at the top of my lungs, but I was counting on my pals from the Luftwaffe not knowing that little trick.

They'd keep their mouths shut like the stoic little members of the Master Race that they envisioned themselves to be, and hopefully they'd pass out. The screaming and shouting isn't from fear: it's to keep your ears and sinuses open, and if you don't do it, you black out more often than not. Someday they'll invent a pressurized pilot's cabin, but until they do, this is the only sure way to keep awake when you're doing a power rise or a lot of looping.

I went straight up to five thousand feet, then, still yelling, killed the power and let the plane spin, tail first, toward the ground. I kicked on the ignition at two thousand feet, but I must have fallen to within fifty feet before I pulled out of it. I finally checked behind me and found that both Messerschmidts had crashed—but just as I was telling myself what a bright young feller I was, four more Messerschmidts appeared and took up the pursuit.

I led them a merry chase, but they were a hell of a lot

faster than me, and within a few minutes I saw that my
chance of getting away unscathed was just about zero.
Besides, I didn't want to get away; all that would mean
was that I'd have to come back to Obersalzberg again,
and this time they'd really be ready for me. Once they
figured out that we were after the V-2, they were going
to throw every top flier they had into its defense.

I put some plastic explosives in my knapsack, made
sure my parachute was buckled on securely, and took
my plane over a nearby forest. I was just over the trees
when I felt the right wing take about four bullets. The
tail went next, and then one of the propellers. By this
time the plane was throwing out the telltale trail of black
smoke that meant it was going down, and I hit the door.
For a minute I thought it wasn't going to open, but
finally it did and I bailed out at about eight thousand
feet.

I knew the Nazis would be trying to nail me as well as
the plane, so I didn't pull the ripcord right away. I tried
to ride the wind currents as best I could, trying to
maneuver my body over a large clearing in the middle of
the Bavarian forest.

Finally, at two thousand feet, I jerked the cord, the
parachute ballooned open, and they finally got a bead
on me. But it was too late for them. A couple of tracer
bullets came within a hundred feet or so of me, but then
I was hidden by the trees. I damned near impaled myself
on a huge broken branch about fifty feet above the
ground, but I twisted my body at the last minute and
avoided it.

The parachute caught on it, though, and an instant
later I found myself hanging about thirty feet above the
ground. It was a grim situation. I'm no coward, but I
sure as hell wasn't going to jump thirty feet to the
ground; the army needed a live saboteur, not a crippled
hero.

I knew I had to act fast. The Messerschmidts would
radio the Nazi base at Obersalzberg that I was in the
woods, and they'd have their ground troops into the
forest in a mere handful of minutes.

I pulled a jackknife out of my pocket, began sawing at the cord, and when only one canvas strap remained unsevered I wrapped it around my hand and pulled myself up its length until I lay panting on the broken branch. From there it was a relatively easy matter to edge myself to the bole of the tree and start shinnying down it. The trunk got too wide about fifteen feet above the ground and I fell the rest of the way, but falling fifteen feet is a far cry from falling thirty, and I picked myself up without any serious damage having been done.

I thought I heard a slight noise, like a cracking twig, behind me, but when I drew my pistol and turned to face it I could see nothing. Writing it off to nerves, I adjusted my backpack and began walking, determined to find some better shelter before the Nazi troops arrived. But it had evidently taken me longer to get out of the tree than I had thought, because I hadn't walked fifty feet when I heard a voice telling me, in German, to halt.

I turned and saw three Nazi soldiers about two hundred feet away. I raised my hands slowly, trying to figure out what to do next. There was no way they were going to take me alive. I may be tough, but I didn't know if I could stand up to the Gestapo's questioning, and I was fully prepared to die before giving them any knowledge of the Allies' espionage activities.

Suddenly there was a blur of motion off to my left, just where I had heard the cracking sound a few moments ago. A girl—an incredibly lovely girl—burst into view and started running toward me.

"Jamie!" called a strong masculine voice.

"He's one of ours!" shouted the girl without looking back. "We've got to help him!"

One of the Nazis whirled and trained his rifle on her, but he collapsed as though pounded by an invisible sledgehammer. Then two tall young men stepped into view, trained odd-looking hand weapons on the two remaining Nazis, and fired. I want to say "pulled the triggers," but I didn't see any triggers. I didn't hear any explosions either, but the two Germans fell to earth just like the first one had.

"Jamie!" snapped the taller of the two men. "What's gotten into you? We're not supposed to get involved!"

The girl had reached me by this time. In fact, I don't think she even knew that the Nazis had been shot down.

"It's all right!" she said breathlessly. "I'm an American!"

"Sure," I said, wondering where she had come from and what she was doing here. "And I'm Bugs Bunny."

"I'm serious," she said, brushing her dark hair out of her eyes. "We just landed here ourselves."

I leveled my gun at her.

"Lady, I may be dumb, but I ain't stupid!" I snarled. "Who are you, and don't give me that hogwash about being an American!"

"But I *am*!" she insisted.

Her two companions were approaching at a trot, and I'd seen enough of their weird weapons to know my pistol wasn't likely to be a match for them, so I grabbed the girl, whirled her around in front of me, put one arm around her neck, and placed the muzzle of my pistol to her temple with my other hand.

"One more step and I'll blow the top of her head off!" I yelled.

They froze.

"Okay," I said. "Suppose you tell me who you are and what you're doing here?"

"You wouldn't understand," said the taller one.

"Try me."

"Look, we just subdued three German soldiers. Shouldn't that act as a show of good faith?"

"I've known the Gestapo to kill one of their own just to gain acceptance and infiltrate an underground group," I said. "You'll have to do better than that."

"My name is Jamie Hamilton," said the girl. "I'm an American reporter. I was born in Glencoe, Illinois."

"Who's the last White Sox pitcher to throw a no-hitter?" I asked.

"How should I know?" she said. "Billy Pierce? Joel Horlen?"

"Never heard of them, lady," I said. "It was Bill Deitrich. A nice German name. You should have known that."

"I'm not a German," she said. "Won't you please let go and listen to me?"

"No way," I said. One of the men took a tentative step toward me and I cocked the pistol. "I'm not kidding!" I yelled. "I'll kill her here and now!"

"There are more Germans coming," said the shorter one. "They'll be here any minute."

"When I want to hear a good story, I'll turn on the radio," I said. "You saved my ass from the Nazis, which is why I haven't killed you yet, but I've got to know who you are and what you're doing here."

"Espionage," said the girl.

"Come on, lady," I said. "When did an espionage team ever take a reporter with them?"

"It's too complicated to explain," she said. "Just let me go and let's get out of here before—"

Suddenly half a dozen Nazis broke into the clearing. The two guys, cool as cucumbers, turned their silent handguns on them, and all six fell like a sack of rocks.

"*Now* can we get out of here?" said the girl.

Well, what was I gonna do? They'd pulled my fat out of the fire twice. Even if they weren't Americans, they sure didn't act like Nazis, and I had to trust somebody, so I nodded and let her go.

"Good," said the taller of the two men. "My name is Troy, and this is Dillon."

"And I'm Jamie," said the girl. "Now let's scram!"

I followed the three of them into the forest. They seemed to know where they were going, and after a couple of miles the trees thinned out and we came to a large farm field.

"About here, weren't they?" asked the one called Dillon.

Troy checked some gadget he was wearing on his

wrist, then shook his head. "About fifty yards to the left."

"What are you talking about?" I said. "I don't see anything!"

"You're not supposed to," said Troy.

"What are you doing here?" said Dillon to me.

"None of your business," I said. "Thanks for helping me out, but I've got to be going. I've got a lot of work to do, and I can do it a lot better alone."

"Jamie?" said Troy.

"As I recall," said Jamie, "the American and Royal Air Forces worked independently except for a few special missions involving spies and sabotage. I think they started collaborating at Peenemunde, which was the first V-1 rocket base."

"Hey!" I said. "You're not supposed to know that! And what's all this crap about recalling, as if this all happened years ago? This is the closest kept Allied secret."

"So if he's really an American, and he was in a British plane," continued the girl, "then he's probably here to sabotage the V-2."

"Good," said Troy. "We're prepared to help you, Colonel . . .?"

"Guidry," I said. "Colonel John Guidry. And I don't need any help!"

"You need all you can get," said Dillon with a smile. "Or do you forget who just saved your life a couple of times?"

"I'm mulling on that," I said slowly. "But who are you guys? The Allies don't have any weapons like the ones you're carrying."

"It's too long to explain," said Troy. "Just believe us: we're on your side."

"I'll settle for your not being on the other side," I said, "and for your forgetting that you ever saw me."

"No chance," said Jamie. "You can't succeed without their help."

"I've been training for this mission for two years," I said. "I probably can't make it *with* their help. I work alone. Thanks for the offer, but just go your own way and don't butt in.''

"And he's one of the Good Guys?" said Troy, shaking his head with an unbelieving smile.

"What's that supposed to mean, wise guy?" I snapped.

I reached for my gun, but before I could pull it from my holster Troy had knocked me flat on my back and Dillon was holding one of those weird weapons on me.

"Let me put it this way," said Troy, his expression unchanged. "Either you work with us or your mission is over."

Mama Guidry may have raised some silly kids, but she didn't produce any suicidal ones. I agreed to let them come along, at least until I could figure out a way to get my hands on one of their crazy pistols.

19

When our men did not return within the hour, I sent
Oberleutnant Branham out with a detail of thirty men
to look for them. All were found lying unconscious at
two locations in the woods. There were no signs of
violence, nor any marks on their bodies. Upon regaining
consciousness they adhered to the wildest imaginable
fantasy to explain their failure to capture the Allied
flier. They showed no signs of drunkenness, but I am
convinced that, for whatever reason, they have dis-
graced the uniforms of the Third Reich.

Recommendations:

J. Huber: Transfer to the Russian front.

W. Blumenstritt: Transfer to the Russian front.

L. Steinhardt: Transfer to the Russian front.

W. Kappstadt: Transfer to the Russian front.

J. Streck: Transfer to the Russian front.

T. Staunning: Transfer to the Russian front.

L. Blaumann: Transfer to the Russian front.

P. Plaga: Transfer to the Russian front.

J. Gansz, officer commanding: Immediate court martial.

Respectfully submitted on
this 4th day of June, 1944

Gen. Wilhelm Yodel

20

They made a motley crew: an American soldier of
1944, an American reporter of 1980, and two warriors
from a distant galaxy. They remained in hiding until
sunset, then made their way into Obersalzberg, keeping
to the shadows and remaining hidden from view.

"My contact is at Number Three Morganstrasse,"
said Guidry. "I'm not supposed to get in touch with her
unless it's an emergency, but our information says that
the V-2 won't be tested until late tomorrow afternoon,
and I sure as hell don't see any way of remaining un-
discovered for twenty hours without help."

"Is your contact in the Underground, or is it another
Allied agent?" asked Jamie.

"Underground," said Guidry. He looked up. "Well,
the moon's gone behind a cloud. We might as well take
a crack at it now. Morganstrasse's two blocks past that
railroad yard," he said, indicating a large depot.

The four took a step out of the shadows. Then Troy
held out an arm and gestured them back.

"What is it?" asked Jamie.

"I don't know," said Troy. "But half a dozen
vehicles are pulling up to the station."

"Troop movment, I suppose," said Guidry.

"I doubt it," said Troy. "There aren't very many
soldiers."

The four of them peered into the darkness. Six large trucks were unloading hundreds of people, each of whom wore a large star somewhere on their clothing.

"Those are Jews," whispered Jamie. "They're being shipped off to concentration camps. Most of them will be killed there."

"Women and children too?" said Troy. "What could they have done to deserve that?"

"Nothing," said Jamie. "They're part of what Hitler called the Final Solution. He needed a scapegoat, a group against which all his dissidents could vent their fears and rage. It's a simple matter of psychology: give them a common enemy to hate and they tend to over-look the fact that you're doing a terrible job of running the country. The economy was in terrible shape when Hitler took over, so he blamed the Jews, many of whom were in the banking and finance business. Also, Ger-many had come out of World War One in such wretched condition that his people had lost most of their self-respect as a nation; by convincing them that the Jews were an inferior people, it automatically upped their own self-esteem. Then, when the war began going badly, he blamed a lot of it on the Jewish underground. None of it was true, from beginning to end, but it was a diabolical way of uniting his people, and to a great degree it worked."

"If this is what they do to innocent people," spat Dillon, "maybe we ought to let Xaviar do his worst here in Germany."

"No!" said Jamie harshly. "Those men with swastikas —twisted crosses—on their armbands are the kind of people he'd be bringing to power throughout the world."

"Who is this Xaviar that you guys are after?" asked Guidry. "Gestapo?"

"Galactican," said Jamie.

"You're making me very uneasy with all this strange terminology," said Guidry. "What's a Galactican?"

"I'll explain it all later," said Jamie. "Right now we've got to help those people on the train."

"We can't, Jamie," said Troy. "Remember your rice example."

"But I can't just stand by and watch them all get carted off to the camps," said Jamie. "You don't know what they were like: Auschwitz, Buchenwald, Dachau . . . Some of them were geared to kill 20,000 people a week!"

"We can't interfere," said Troy firmly.

"But we've got to!" said Jamie. "I don't care what it does to history! We've got to do something!"

"I think she's flipped her wig," said Guidry.

"No," said Troy. "She's just forgotten a few very important facts."

As they spoke in the shadows, a little girl, no more than four years old, crawled out from under one of the trucks, frightened and alone. Her parents had already been loaded into the train, and after a moment of fearful indecision, she began running away from the trucks.

"She's coming right at us!" whispered Dillon.

A guard noticed her and gestured to two of his companions. They began trotting after her.

"She's leading them right toward us!" said Guidry. "We've got to get out of here."

Troy drew his hand weapon and set it to stun. Then, turning to Dillon, he said: "You get the girl, I'll take care of the soldiers."

Dillon nodded, and as the girl raced past them he reached out and grabbed her, simultaneously clasping his hand over her mouth to stifle her scream of fear and surprise.

As Dillon grabbed the girl, Troy leaped out into the street, leveled his weapon at the three guards, and fired it. They collapsed in their tracks, but other soldiers had seen them fall and began running toward Troy.

"Dillon, get them to Guidry's contact. I'll meet you there later."

"Three Morganstrasse," said Dillon, taking Jamie by the hand and starting to run off into the darkness.

"You can't leave him at their mercy!" said Jamie, pulling back.

"Believe me, Jamie," whispered Dillon urgently. "Those Germans have got a lot more to fear from Troy than he has to fear from them. Now let's get going!"

He raced off, the girl under his arm, followed by Jamie and Guidry.

Troy showed himself, then ran in an opposite direction from his companions, stunning five more Germans in the process. Soon the train and trucks were forgotten, and the seventy remaining Nazis began encircling the young warrior. Two shots that missed his head by inches sent pieces of brick flying into his face and he darted into an alley between two buildings.

Four Germans reached the alley a moment later, and he felled them with his sidearm. Then, holstering it, he raced through the alley, emerging at the other end just in time to run into three more Germans.

They were as startled as he was, but Troy's reflexes were quicker. He slashed the first German in the neck with the edge of his hand, ducked a blow from the second, gave a quick kick to the solar plexus of the third, and then hurled himself at the second. The man fell backward with Troy on top of him. His head thudded against the ground, and despite the protection of his helmet he immediately lost consciousness.

The noise of the scuffle had brought more troops, and Troy darted into a nearby building. Taking the stairs four at a time he was on the third floor in a matter of seconds. From here he looked out a window and saw that a large number of the Nazi soldiers were converging on the building.

With a confident smile Troy reached for the switch that activated his personal invisibility shield—and discovered that the controls had been damaged during his brief scuffle with the three soldiers. His energizer wasn't depleted, which meant that the field still worked, but he had no way to turn it on.

He raced back into the hallway, climbed another flight of stairs, and lifted a skylight that allowed him access to the roof. Before the Germans knew he was there he had raced the length of the rooftop and leaped through space to an adjacent roof some twenty-five feet distant.

"There he is!" cried a voice, and a hail of bullets cascaded around him. He hit the deck, waited until the guns had stopped after a few seconds, then abruptly stood up and swept the area around the building with his weapon set on stun. Five more soldiers dropped in their tracks, but the remainder started firing again, and he ran to a door leading to the interior of the building.

It was an old, dilapidated apartment house, and he soon found a door leading to a four-room flat. He kicked it open, quickly stunned the man and woman who began screaming for help when he entered, and began rummaging through their closets. He found a tattered overcoat and a battered fedora, put them on over his clothes, and ran out into the hallway, where he descended to the first floor. He heard a number of soldiers entering and backed away.

"He must still be in here!" said one of them.

"All right," said another voice. "We'll proceed methodically. Schlutter, you take four men up to the top floor and begin working your way down. The rest of you men, check all the apartments on the main floor and then proceed up the stairs. And be careful! I don't know what kind of gun he's got, but he's disabled more than a dozen men so far between that weapon and his physical prowess."

Troy waited until five soldiers began climbing the stairs, and others had entered the various main floor apartments. Only one man remained on guard and Troy finally stepped out into the hall, in full sight of the soldier.

The man whirled, trying to level his gun at the warrior, but Troy was quicker, striking him with a blow that would have felled an ox.

"Help!" Troy cried, and soon the corridor was filled with soldiers.

"A strange man struck this officer and then ran out the doorway," said Troy in perfect German. "He had a strange-looking pistol in his hand."

"Which way did he go?" demanded an officer.

Troy shrugged his shoulders. "I don't know. Everything happened so fast."

The Nazis raced out the door, leaving one man behind in case the intruder returned. Troy waited until they were out of sight, then dropped the man with a quick chop to the back of the neck, and began searching for a rear exit. He found it, kept to the shadows for a couple of blocks, and then, pulling the fedora down over his face, he stepped to the middle of the sidewalk and began looking for Morganstrasse.

He had walked perhaps half a mile when two German officers called after him to halt. He did so and turned to face them.

"You, there!" said one of them.

He indicated himself questioningly.

"Yes, you! What are you doing out at this time of night? Don't you know there's a curfew? Let me see your papers."

"Papers?" repeated Troy.

"Don't be so dense," snapped the higher-ranking of the two. "Your identification papers."

"I must have left them in my apartment," said Troy.

Both men drew their pistols immediately.

"Come with us!" snapped one of them.

"You insist?" said Troy.

His answer was a guttural curse.

He shrugged, pretended to take a step in the direction they had indicated, and quickly drew and fired his sidearm. Both men fell to the pavement before they could utter a sound and Troy dragged them into a nearby building.

"This isn't exactly the greatest town in the world to be a civilian in," he muttered, stripping one of them and donning his clothes. "But soldiers seem to come and go unchallenged." He pulled out the man's I.D. photo and wallet. "Sergeant Josef Lammers," he mused. "An officer would have been even better, but beggars can't be choosers."

He tied and gagged the two men securely, deposited

them in a darkened basement, and soon was walking through the city again, once more seeking Morganstrasse. It took him about half an hour to find it, and a few minutes more to come to the door of Number Three.

He knocked twice, then waited.

After a long moment a light went on and a wizened old woman came to the door.

"Yes?" she said.

"Excuse me for intruding," he said, "but I believe that three of my friends are at this address."

"There's nobody here but me," said the woman coldly.

"Don't let my uniform scare you," he said. "Their names are Dillon, Jamie and John."

"Nothing scares me any more," said the old crone. "And I repeat: no one's here."

"I don't want to hurt you or to force my way in here," said Troy, switching to English. "Why not do me a favor, and tell the one named Dillon that Serena's son would like to speak to him?"

"I know no one named Dillon."

Troy considered stunning her, but she was so old and frail and shrivelled that he wasn't sure she could survive the shock, so he settled for gently lifting her by the shoulders and setting her back down a few feet to the left. Then, smiling at her, he walked calmly through the doorway.

And, smiling at him, she pulled a wicked-looking knife out of her sleeve and thrust it into his belly.

He uttered a surprised grunt, clutched his stomach, and collapsed in a heap at her feet.

21

At first his body seemed to be one gigantic ache. Then, as he opened his eyes, he was able to distinguish the different agonies: the pain in his abdomen, the throbbing of his head (which, he concluded, must have banged into the floor when he fell), the dizziness that still remained even after his eyes began focusing.

Jamie was bending over him, mopping his forehead, and Dillon was looking at him with a worried expression on his face.

"What happened?" asked Troy.

"We told our hostess to be on the lookout for you, but we didn't tell her you'd be in a Nazi storm trooper's outfit," said Dillon. "She thought the Germans had captured you and sent someone in your place."

The old crone walked over. "I am sorry," she said in a cracked voice that sounded every bit as old as she looked. "It was all my fault."

"It's all right," said Troy. "You couldn't have known."

"I am forgiven?" asked the old woman.

"There's nothing to forgive," said Troy, rolling over slightly in an effort to get more comfortable.

"Troy," said Dillon, "let me introduce you to Ramona Brandhorst. She owns this building, and she'll be letting us stay here until we have to meet Xaviar."

"My house is yours," said the old woman. "But it would be much safer for you in the attic. If the Nazis come, you're too weak to move in a hurry."

"You're right, Ramona," said Troy, gesturing Dillon and Guidry to help him to his feet. The pain was excruciating, but he merely grimaced and refused to utter a sound. "If we could only get the MedKit from the Viper . . ." he said, his voice trailing off.

"I have medicine," said Ramona.

"It's not as good as ours," said Dillon. "Maybe I ought to sneak back and pick it up."

"No," said Troy. "It was hard enough to get here a first time. No sense taking extra chances that might give us away."

"Right," said Dillon, leading Troy up to the attic. "Ramona tells me there's a cot up there. You lay down and try to get some sleep. I'll stand watch downstairs."

"All right," said Troy, consciousness escaping from him again. "And Dillon—no heroics."

"Of course not," said Dillon, crossing his fingers behind his back.

22

"Jamie," said Dillon, descending the stairs, "keep an eye on Troy. I've got to get back to the Viper."

"But it's miles away!" protested Jamie.

"No choice," said Dillon. "That's a mighty big hole in his belly, and the bleeding's started again."

"Isn't there some alternative?"

"How?" said Dillon. "You can't tie a tourniquet around a stomach. And what doctor in this town will treat him without making a full report to the Nazis?"

"What have you got on the Viper?"

"A MedKit that'll clean and suture his wound in a matter of minutes, and drugs that will prevent infection more thoroughly than your primitive penicillin can do. And I've got some amphetamines that will help him function efficiently tomorrow. He's lost a lot of blood, and he's in mild shock; even if some local patched him up, we'd have to carry him to the Viper on a stretcher tomorrow. What do you think our chances of getting there unscathed would be?"

"Will you be all right?" she asked, lines of worry crossing her pretty face.

"Sure," said Dillon. "I've got my invisibility field." He switched it on and promptly vanished. "Nothing to it," he said. "I'll leave it on all the way there and back, and I'll be back here with the MedKit in less than an hour.''

"Good luck," she said, walking him to the door.

A moment later he was out in the street, and within thirty minutes he had found the Vipers. He withdrew a MedKit and began walking back to town.

"Halt!" cried a voice when he was within about three blocks of Ramona Brandhorst's house. He kept on walking, and was surprised to feel a firm hand on his shoulder a few seconds later.

"Did you not hear my command?" said a German lieutenant.

Dillon's jaw fell. He looked down and saw—*himself*. Then he remembered Doctor Zee's warning, that even a small invisibility field took an enormous amount of power. Evidently his energizer had run down, and he hadn't even been aware of it until the German had spotted him.

"I'm sorry, Lieutenant," he said in German. "I am a little hard of hearing. I truly did not hear you."

The lieutenant looked him up and down, obviously comparing him with a description of Troy. Finally he shrugged. "Pay more attention in the future. Now let me see your papers and you can be on your way."

"I left them at home," said Dillon.

"We are under martial law," said the officer. "You must produce your papers or come back to the base with me."

"Well, possibly I do have them," said Dillon. "Let me search my pockets." He reached into a pocket, withdrew a hand weapon, and fired. The officer collapsed without a sound.

Dillon quickly examined his alternatives. He could continue walking boldly along as if he had every right to be on the streets—but Obersalzberg was a small town, and it was doubtful that he could cover the remaining three blocks without being stopped again, and it wouldn't do to stun too many policemen near Number Three Morganstrasse. After all, Ramona Brandhorst had to live here after he and Troy and Jamie were gone.

He could simply wait until daylight and then try to get to the apartment house while the townspeople were scurrying to work—but Troy needed the medication *now*. And besides, there was no guarantee that he wouldn't be stopped, if not by the soldiers, then by some of the loyal citizens who knew all the town's inhabitants and would know that he was not one of them.

So he chose what seemed to him the only viable alternative, and began sneaking furtively through the shadows, stopping in a building's outer court, skulking down an alley, pausing for long minutes before attempting to cross any streets or walk under any streetlamps. He did not approach the house directly, but took a very circuitous route. Within forty minutes he was on Morganstrasse, a block away from his destination. Then, waiting long enough to make sure there were no Nazi soldiers in the vicinity, he walked boldly down the middle of the sidewalk. He was within twenty feet of the front door when a neighbor stuck his head out of a second-story window and shouted: "Who are you! Why are you out in the street? Officers! Officers! Spy!"

"Damn!" muttered Dillon. He broke into a run and raced past Ramona Brandhorst's building. Four buildings farther down the block he cut between two apartment houses, ducking out of sight just as he heard a score of troops running up the street.

He crouched down between two garbage cans, his back propped up against the wall of a building, and waited. Ordinarily the Nazis would probably search for a few minutes and then assume that the neighbor had merely given in to an overactive imagination. But not today, not after he and Troy had saved Guidry and immobilized nine officers in the woods, and especially not after Troy had single-handedly fought his way out of a certain deathtrap.

So he waited, ten, twenty, forty minutes. The footsteps grew dim and distant. He waited another ten minutes, just to be on the safe side, then slowly, carefully, his back sliding against the wall, he edged his way toward the street. There was only one soldier in sight.

He checked the moon. It was late, very late now, and the sun would be coming up before too long. If he waited any longer too many people would be out on the street. If he was ever to get back to Troy's bedside with the MedKit he had to do it now.

Then his eyes fell on the soldier. The man had six hand grenades strung around his belt. Dillon had never seen a grenade explode, but he was easily able to analyze how it worked—and he suddenly knew that he couldn't take the chance of stunning the soldier from this distance. If the man fell wrong, two or three of the grenades could detach themselves from his belt and explode, and that would bring the whole command post down on his neck in a matter of minutes, possibly seconds.

Carefully, softly, he removed the MedKit from his back and placed it down on the ground, just out of sight around the corner of the building that was shielding him. Then, catlike, he moved in a silent crouching run. He ducked behind a stone staircase when he was about fifty feet distant from the soldier, and held so motionless that he barely even breathed. He looked ahead. There was a lone tree for cover between himself and the soldier, and he waited until the soldier turned his back and darted for the tree.

He made it, still unseen and unheard. But now he knew further stealth was out of the question. Once again he crouched, like some huge, muscular beast of prey ready to spring, and waited.

The soldier lit a cigarette, threw the match into a wet gutter, and began walking in Dillon's direction. He stopped about twelve feet from the tree, turned to go back as if he had forgotten something, then shrugged, took another puff, and turned back toward the tree.

Dillon took one more huge gulp of air and leaped out from cover. He crossed the intervening space between himself and the soldier in two long strides and had thrown the man on his back before the fellow knew what had hit him.

The soldier tried to scream, and Dillon put a huge hand over his mouth and leaned. The soldier responded by sticking a thumb in Dillon's left eye and clawing at his face with his other hand.

Dillon tried to draw his head back out of the way, but he couldn't do that and still keep the soldier quiet. He took his free hand and squeezed the soldier's throat with all the power he possessed.

The soldier's body began jerking and he redoubled his efforts to separate Dillon's eye from his head. They remained motionless, each wondering if the other would ever give in, when suddenly the soldier jerked spasmodically one more time and his whole body relaxed. Dillon rolled off him, rubbed his eye, and then checked to make sure he hadn't killed the soldier.

The man was breathing, shallowly but regularly, and Dillon ran back, picked up the MedKit, and a moment later was once again inside Ramona Brandhorst's building.

"What kept you?" demanded Jamie as he took the MedKit up the stairs to the attic.

"Just lazy, I guess," he said, trying to force a carefree grin.

"What happened to your eye?" asked Guidry.

"Nothing much," said Dillon. "Why?"

"It's bleeding, and the flesh around it is discolored," said Guidry, following the two of them up the stairs.

"Lucky I've got the MedKit then, isn't it?" said Dillon.

He entered the attic room. Troy was out cold, completely oblivious to the world. Dillon took the bandages and gauze off Troy's stomach, pulled out a molecular cauterizer, laid it down next to the bed, then found the disinfectant he was looking for.

"Might as well add a little viruscide to the germicide," he muttered. He injected a small amount of solution into Troy's arm, sprayed the area around the cut which was already turning a nasty-looking shade of blue, and applied the cauterizer to the wound. It sealed without leaving a noticeable mark, and he then injected Troy with a solution that was part steroid, part amphetamine, part antibiotic, and part phenylbutazone.

A moment later Troy opened his eyes. He felt his stomach, then swung his legs to the floor and sat up on his cot.

"You went back," he said accusingly.

"I had to," said Dillon. "I'm going to win so many honors and medals for stopping Xaviar that I'll need help carrying them around."

"Thanks," said Troy. "Any trouble?"

"Nothing I couldn't handle."

"Is that why your eye looks so good?" said Troy with a smile.

"I'd forgotten all about it," said Dillon. "Have you got a mirror?"

"You're a heck of a fighter, Dillon, but you've always had a queasy stomach," said Troy. "Do yourself a favor and don't look in a mirror until I fix you up." He began going through the MedKit until he found what he needed, and a moment later Dillon's eye was as good as new again.

"Well, what now?" asked Troy, standing and stretching.

"Now," said Guidry, standing in the doorway with his pistol trained on Troy, Dillon and Jamie, "we talk."

"What's this all about?" asked Jamie.

"I saw what these two guys just did to each other, lady, and Uncle Sam hasn't got anything like that in his medicine bag. So you're finally going to tell me what's going on here, or your adventure is going to come to a very unhappy end on the count of three."

He cocked the trigger.

23

I held the gun on them and waited.

Finally Troy spoke up. "We're from what you might call a planetwide organization. More than that I'm not at liberty to tell you. A member of our organization, a man named Xaviar, has defected to the Nazis. You've seen some of our equipment, you know how technologically advanced it is. You'll have to take my word that we possess weapons that make the standard bomb look like a child's firecracker. Our mission is to get to Xaviar and stop him before he turns the secrets of these weapons over to the Nazis."

"No group I know of has weapons, or even medicine, like you people," I said, not lowering the gun or taking my eyes off them for an instant. "I know enough German to know your German is flawless; so's your English. Where are you from and exactly what nations do you represent?"

"They've pulled your fat out of the fire," said Jamie. "Isn't that enough?"

"No," I said coldly. "I'm used to giving orders, not taking them. If I'm going to keep doing what these two guys tell me to do, I've got to know who they are and why I should obey them."

"We simply can't tell you any more," said Troy calmly. "If you knew the truth it would have too great

118

an influence on your future actions, and those actions must follow a certain set pattern.''

"I don't know what you're talking about," I said, "and furthermore, this is war. So far everything you've done seems like you're on our side, but I can't be sure, and if I can't be sure than I can't trust you with my life or my mission's success. There are some gaps in your behavior, too, and I've got to know about them.''

"Such as?" said Dillon.

"Such as why you wouldn't lift a finger to help the Jews who were being loaded onto the train. Why you won't kill any Nazis, but are content to temporarily disable them. Why a White Sox fan doesn't know who Bill Deitrich is.''

"We aren't here to help or harm anyone," said Troy. "Our directions and mission are quite specific. We are here to stop Xaviar from aiding the Nazis. Nothing more, nothing less.''

"But you won't do a damned thing to the Nazis themselves," I persisted. "Why?''

"I can't tell you," said Troy.

"I'm only going to ask you one more time," I said meaningfully.

"You're going to have to shoot, then," said Troy. "I've told you all that I can.''

I pointed the gun at his chest and began squeezing the trigger. Then, no more than half a second before the gun would have fired, I heard the little Jewish girl scream, and the sounds of the front door being broken.

"We'll settle this later," I said, running out of the attic and leaning over the rail at the head of the stairs. The little girl was racing up the stairs, screaming in panic, with a trio of storm troopers hot on her trail. I leveled the gun at them, then felt Dillon's hand on my own.

"No," he whispered. "Too noisy.''

He aimed his own weapon at them. There was a little hum of power, and the three troopers dropped their weapons and tumbled back down the stairs, senseless.

Jamie lifted the girl up in her arms and took her back

into the attic, but I knew we weren't out of danger yet, because I could hear the sounds of a lot more soldiers walking around the main floor. They were speaking harshly with Ramona Brandhorst, who took up her blind-deaf-and-sullen old lady act with them.

I went back to the attic.

"We've had it," I announced softly. "There must be a dozen of them talking to the old lady right now. Any second they're going to see those bodies on the stairs."

"That's bad," mused Troy. "We don't want to draw any further attention to ourselves."

"You don't understand," I said, exasperated. "We're trapped like rats up here! There's no exit and they're going to take us like shooting fish in a barrel."

"No sense stunning them," said Dillon, totally ignoring me. "They'll just send more."

"Damn it!" I said. "Doesn't anyone know what I'm talking about?"

"Be quiet, Guidry," said Troy distractedly. "They'll be up here soon enough as it is, without your shouting."

"My energizer's on zero," said Dillon.

"And my controls are broken," said Troy. "Have we got enough time to transfer my energizer to your field?"

"I doubt it," said Dillon.

"Wait, you guys," said Jamie. "I've got a field too, you know. Adama gave it to me before we left."

"I know, Jamie," said Troy. "But it won't encompass the three of us plus Guidry and the child."

"How many *will* it hold?" she said.

"If we're very very lucky, it might shield three of us plus the child."

"Fields and shields?" I said. "What the hell are you talking about? Draw your guns and get ready to sell your lives as dearly as possible."

"Do shut up, Colonel Guidry," said Jamie impatiently. "We've got a serious decision to make."

"There's no decision at all," I snapped. "Let's take as many of these Nazi bastards with us as we can!"

"Primitives!" said Dillon, looking at me and shaking

his head sadly. "What are you going to do with them? They're all alike!"

"This gun fires in all directions," I said ominously.

"Has it ever occurred to you to use your brain instead of your brawn?" said Dillon.

"Quiet, Dillon," said Troy. "We've still got a decision ahead of us. I think I should let them take me."

"Take you!" I said. "What are you talking about?"

"If you use Jamie's field, it'll only take you an hour or so to get back to the Viper, charge your own energizer, and then come back and get me out of wherever they put me. But my controls are broken; if they take you, I still could only bring one useful screen back."

"I see your point," said Dillon. He gestured to me. "Come over here, Guidry, and stand as close to Jamie and me as you can."

"To hell with you!" I snapped, peeking out the door. "Let 'em come on up after us—I'm ready!"

"Colonel Guidry," said Dillon, "if you don't do as you're told I'm going to come over and break your arm."

I spun back to him, prepared to tell him where he could shove his idiot orders, and found myself staring at that weird handgun. With a sigh I raised my hands and moved where he gestured me.

"Good luck, Troy," said Jamie.

"Thanks," he said.

And then Jamie touched something on her belt, and suddenly we were absolutely invisible! I held my hand up to my eyes and could see right through it!

Troy walked over to the doorway, stepped out to the head of the stairs, and cleared his throat. Ten seconds later he was surrounded by Nazis.

"I've been waiting for you," he said calmly.

24

"Your name?"

"Troy."

"Rank?"

"Captain."

"Serial number?"

"None."

CRACK!

"Serial number!"

"None."

"Are you American?"

"No."

"English?"

"No."

CRACK!

"American?"

"No."

"English?"

"No."

CRACK!

"What is your assignment in Obersalzberg?"

Silence.

CRACK!

"What are you doing in Obersalzberg?"

"Answering your questions."

CRACK!

"What is your connection with the woman Ramona Brandhorst?"

"Who?"

"Ramona Brandhorst."

"I've never heard of her."

"Who told you to go to Number Three Morgan-strasse?"

"No one."

"Then why were you there?"

"It was a chilly night, and I—"

CRACK!

"Oberleutnant Branham," said a new voice. "I believe that this is the man who caused the commotion during the decampment proceedings."

"Were you at the railroad station earlier today?" said the now-familiar voice of Branham as the questioning continued.

Troy blinked his eyes, tears streaming down his cheeks from the blindingly bright lights that were focused on him.

"Yes, I was."

"And you attacked German soldiers?"

"No."

CRACK!

"And you attacked German soldiers?"

"No. They attacked me. I merely defended myself."

"And incapacitated more than thirty of them," said Branham.

"If you say so."

"What weapon did you use?"

"I don't understand you."

"The weapon," said Branham. "What was it?"

"I don't know what you mean."

CRACK!

"Where is this weapon?"

No answer.

"Captain Troy, I have very little patience remaining. Where is this weapon?"

Silence.

"Captain Troy, do you see this cigaret I am holding in my hand?"

"I can't see anything. The light is in my eyes."

"Then you will have to accept my word that I am holding a lighted cigaret," said Oberleutnant Branham. "And I now tell you to further accept my word that if you do not immediately tell me where the weapon is, I shall snuff this cigaret out in your left eye. If you still do not tell me who sent you here and where your weapon is, I will light another cigaret. You will have the length of time it takes me to smoke it, perhaps five minutes, certainly no more than seven, and I will then put it out in your right eye. I will ask you just one more time: where is the weapon?"

"What weapon?" said Troy.

"Maybe he means *this* weapon," said a familiar voice.

There was a hum of power and Troy heard two bodies collapse. Then Dillon was untying him and helping him to his feet.

"You cut it awfully close," Troy said, rubbing his burning eyes.

"Sorry," said Dillon, "but it took a little longer to charge my energizer than I thought it would. Are you all right?"

Troy nodded. "I'll be a little stiff and sore until I can get to a MedKit, but I think they were mostly trying to frighten me. The real brutality was still half a minute away."

Dillon handed Troy an energizer and the invisibility field controls.

"What's the situation?" asked Troy.

"I snuck in," said Dillon. "I knew I'd have to subdue a few Nazis once I reached you, and I didn't want to alert them with too much noise on the way in. Bullets hurt, even if they can't see what they're firing at."

"I'm just grateful that the Allies eventually won this war," said Troy. "I'd hate to have to help the Nazis."

"Not real lovable folks," agreed Dillon. "Well, if

you're up to it, let's get moving. There's a corridor to the right, then an open courtyard leading to a heavily guarded gate. Trucks go in and out every five or six minutes, so we'll just wait and walk out when they open the doors."

"Wait a minute," said Troy as Dillon faded from sight. "I don't know where I am."

"I almost forgot," said Dillon. "You're in the Luftwaffe Headquarters, in the southeast section of Obersalzberg. Our Vipers are about six miles due south of here. Once we get out, keep walking along Ravenstrasse for about four blocks, then turn right on what looks like a major thoroughfare leading out of the city. As soon as I'm sure no Nazis are around I'll switch off my field and you can just follow me by sight from there on."

"Lead the way," said Troy, also fading from sight.

25

They returned before sunrise, carrying a number of German uniforms. I asked where they got them, but they just ignored the question and Troy motioned me to put one on.

They kept talking about something called a Viper, or a pair of Vipers, I'm not sure which. These Viper things are obviously very important to them, and they worry about some kind of field flickering off, but it's all Greek to me.

Except that, from various things I've overheard, I got the impression that these Vipers were within a few hundred feet of us—and yet, we were standing in the middle of an empty wheat field! More invisibility, I guess.

When the sun rose we waited a few hours until it seemed to be about noon, then began making our way to the V-2 launching base.

"Is *this* what all the fuss is about?" said Troy incredulously when his eyes finally fell on the rocket. "Just a crude pulse jet?"

What kind of men are these???

26

Yodel was dubious.

Wars were fought with tanks and artillery and foot soldiers. He had lately come to the realization of the major role air power now played in modern warfare, but rockets were still beyond his ken.

He paced back and forth in a bunker near the launching area, occasionally looking out the window at the V-2.

"Considering the price, and the small payload of explosives, it has done very little but frighten a few English civilians," he said at last.

"But that was only the beginning," said Colonel Conrad Werner. "What you will see today is the second generation . . . the V-2 . . . completely programmable to land wherever we want, and to carry a payload that is the beginning of the end for the Allies."

"Bah!" said Yodel. "The Allies will be landing somewhere in France any day now, and we waste soldiers in this forsaken hellhole! And me—a general— they have pulled out of action and placed in charge of Obersalzberg for the past two weeks. I should be with my army, not here looking at the Fuehrer's newest tinkertoy. Why can't that damned Bohemian Corporal leave the fighting to his generals?"

Werner cringed at Yodel's contemptuous description

of Hitler, but said nothing. There had already been one
attempt on the Fuehrer's life; if Yodel were this open
about his dislike of the man, possibly another assassina-
tion plot was in the making. Or possibly the war effort
was going worse than anyone yet suspected. In either
case, he found the general's attitude disquieting.

Yodel turned to Werner. "I am curious about this
defector who seems to have provided us with such a
miraculous breakthrough. Tell me more about him."

"He's an Englishman who has perhaps made a few
minor contributions," said Werner hastily, "but I
assure you, General, that our own scientists would have
reached the same conclusions on their own, in a mere
matter of months."

"When you are losing a war, a few months can make
all the difference," said Yodel.

So it *was* true! The Allies had done much more
damage than his superiors had admitted to. The situation was even more desperate than he had feared.

Suddenly Werner didn't want to be the ranking
officer nearest to General Yodel if the V-2 didn't work
to perfection. There were no higher officers around, but
he *could* send for the Englishman. At least, if anything
went wrong, he could direct Yodel's fury at the turncoat
scientist.

"Have Doctor Xaviar brought to the bunker," said
Werner to an orderly.

"But sir," said the orderly, "he has requested per-
mission to continue working in his laboratory, as usual.
I think he must be a very shy man."

"Get him here *schnell*!" snapped Werner. "Or he's
going to be a very unhappy man!"

•   •   •

"We're going to have to get beyond those trees if
we're going to destroy it," said Guidry.

"What good will destroying a rocket do when they
still have the technology to build more?" asked Dillon
of no one in particular.

"There was a real tug-of-war going on between
various factions of the German military over where to

concentrate the last of their resources and fuels," said Jamie. "But even if we succeed," she continued, puzzled, "the program wasn't cancelled. The Germans did build rockets."

"*Did*?" repeated Guidry. "What are you talking about?"

"But if Xaviar's rocket works, they'll pour everything they have into the V-2," said Troy. "Destroying this rocket will delay their progress for a few months, Earth time."

"Earth time?" said Guidry.

"Figure of speech," said Troy. "Anyway, the Germans aren't supposed to have a functional V-2 rocket in June."

"You guys are crazy!" said Guidry. "As of this moment, I'm taking charge of this operation. You," he said, pointing toward Jamie, "stay here with the kid. You two, follow me."

"I think I'll stay behind too," said Troy. "I'm still a little beat up from last night. I'd only be in the way."

"Suit yourself," shrugged Guidry. "Just don't get in the line of fire. How about you?" he asked Dillon. "Are you coming?"

"I wouldn't miss it for the galaxy," said Dillon with a smile.

The two men set off for the landing field, moving in low, crouching walks.

When they were a few hundred yards away Troy opened the MedKit. He withdrew something that looked vaguely like a syringe, held it to the little girl's arm, and pressed a button. The girl collapsed in Jamie's arms.

"What did you do?" she demanded.

"Just gave her a two-hour nap, nothing more," said Troy reassuringly. "Let's put her in one of the Vipers, where she'll be safe. Then you and I have work to do."

• • •

Xaviar entered the room, his cold gray eyes darting hither and thither. His battered overcoat and German hairstyle couldn't hide a certain contemptuousness, a certain *alienness* to his bearing.

"This is the English scientist, General," said Werner.

Yodel walked over to Xaviar, studying him intently.
"Doctor Xaviar," he said at last, "I understand you
were able to provide us with a few minor aids to our
cause."

"Minor?" said Xaviar haughtily. "I and I alone
made this entire event possible."

"The English are such a modest people," said Yodel
with an amusement he didn't feel.

"Most Englishmen have a lot to be modest about,"
agreed Xaviar coldly. He stepped back as a pair of
technicians placed shields with eye-slits over the
windows.

"It is most curious," said Yodel. "We follow your
scientific ranks quite closely. Yet I don't recall ever
seeing a Doctor Xaviar mentioned as a part of the
British rocket program . . . or any place else, for that
matter."

"Yet here I am," replied Xaviar, staring boldly back
at him. "And the proof of my competence stands on the
launch field out there."

Yodel walked to an eye-slit, looked at the rocket,
frowned, then turned back to Xaviar.

"You may as well know, Doctor Xaviar," he said,
"that were the choice mine I would prefer to build more
tanks, more guns. Dependable weapons of war. But I
am willing to be proven wrong."

"Rest assured, you will be," said Xaviar.

Yodel glared at him for a long moment, then went
back to looking through the eye-slit. As he did so, two
uniformed officers materialized out of thin air at the
rear of the bunker.

Xaviar had been smiling nastily when Yodel walked
away. The smile was wiped off his face as he recognized
the taller of the two officers, to be replaced by a look of
total surprise.

"So, Captain Troy," he whispered, "you were able
to follow me into the past. Very clever—but you're too
late."

"Xaviar, the council orders you to return with me,"

said Troy, keeping his voice low enough so that only Xaviar could hear it.

"I am beyond the council!" hissed Xaviar. "And if you attempt to stop what I've started here, I'll expose you."

"You'll have to find us first," said Troy calmly. A microsecond later he and Jamie had vanished.

Xaviar, unaware of what to expect next, leaned back against a wall of the bunker, his body tense.

"It isn't going to work, Xaviar," said Troy's voice a few inches from his ear.

"It *must* work!" whispered Xaviar. "You know it and I know it: to save our people they must develop their rockets more rapidly. They must have already progressed to magnetic field travel before the onset of the 21st Century."

"You can't tamper with history without killing innocent people," said Troy. "And these people you're trying to help—they're the worst fiends in the history of the planet, more barbaric than the lowest savage."

"It's too late to try to stop me!" snapped Xaviar.

"Did you say something, Doctor Xaviar?" said General Yodel from across the room.

"I was just clearing my throat," said Xaviar.

"You look nervous, Doctor," said Yodel ominously. "I thought success was a foregone conclusion."

"Oh, it is," said Werner, making sure the general knew where he stood on the matter. "Or Doctor Xaviar will have a lot to answer for."

Yodel looked wryly amused. "And I thought you said he contributed so little, Colonel."

"Well, I mean—"

"I know exactly what you mean, Colonel Werner," said Yodel. "And let me say that if the V-2 rocket is unsuccessful, *many* people will have much to answer for. Do I make myself quite clear?"

"Quite, sir," said Werner, swallowing hard.

"All right," said Yodel, turning back to the launching field. "Let's get on with it."

"Two minutes and counting," said a technician.

• • •

Dillon and Guidry squatted in tall grass, about sixty yards from the rocket.

"Look," said Dillon, "I hate to tell you this, but there are two guys right behind us and a bomb about to go off right in front of us."

"I know my job," snapped Guidry.

"Sure," said Dillon. "But what do you know about rockets? They throw an afterburn wide enough to burn you to a crisp."

"NINETY SECONDS AND COUNTING," said a voice over a loudspeaker.

"Okay," whispered Guidry. "When the count reaches sixty seconds I'm gonna take those two Germans out; then I'll go to work with the explosives."

Dillon shook his head disgustedly.

"Didn't you hear me?" he said. "The afterburn radius is—"

"SIXTY SECONDS AND COUNTING."

Guidry stood up, found that the two soldiers were about thirty yards away, and aimed his gun. Dillon rose and, in a single motion, knocked Guidry's gun out of his hand and fired his own weapon at the Germans. They sank slowly to the ground without a sound.

"How did you do that?" demanded Guidry. "Who are you?"

"Isn't it about time you stopped asking questions and started listening to me?"

"When you're programmed to do one job for more than two years, you don't let anyone or anything get in your way," said Guidry, pulling out his explosives. "Take a gander at this stuff. Whatever your unit is, you're not the only one with super weapons."

"What's that?" asked Dillon.

"The latest innovation. They're called plastic explosives. If I can get to the base of that rocket in the next half minute, it's all over."

He took off at a run.

Dillon aimed his weapon at Guidry. It hummed with

power, and the American pitched face-forward onto the ground.

"Primitives!" spat Dillon, pulling Guidry back from the rocket.

"THIRTY SECONDS AND COUNTING."

Dillon dropped to one knee and waited patiently.

"TEN SECONDS . . . NINE . . . EIGHT . . ."

He aimed his weapon at a point three hundred feet above the rocket's nose.

"THREE . . . TWO . . . ONE . . . FIRE!"

The rocket's tail belched forth smoke and flame and it began slowly climbing into the sky. Dillon took careful aim, led it by a few yards, and fired. He made a direct hit—and nothing happened.

He quickly looked down at his controls, and saw that they were still set to stun. Cursing silently, he adjusted the power, took aim again, and fired just as it had climbed to the limit of his field of vision.

The V-2 exploded into a million flaming pieces.

● ● ●

"This man is a spy," said Yodel, turning and indicating Xaviar with a certain amount of satisfaction. "Place him under arrest. As for you, Werner—I'll deal with you later." He threw his overcoat about his shoulders. "And now, if you all will excuse me, I have an important phone call to make to Berlin."

"General, I don't know what went wrong," said Werner, his face drenched in sweat, his hands balled up into tight little fists. "But it did work . . . you saw it work."

"I saw four million deutsch marks rise a few hundred yards into the air and then turn into a pile of scrap metal," said Yodel coldly. "What do you propose to do with a rocket that flies less than a mile, Colonel Werner? Ask the British if they would mind moving a little closer?"

He turned on his heel and left.

"Well, don't just stand there!" yelled Werner. "Take the English spy out of here!"

Troy saluted, moved quickly to Xaviar, beating a couple of other officers who were approaching the Galactican, and took him by the shoulder. As he walked to the door, Jamie joined him and took Xaviar's other arm.

"But rockets *will* work!" said Werner, staring out at the launching area. "We will have to spend more time, but they will work."

"Sure they will," whispered one orderly to another. "And someday we'll land on the moon as well!"

It was all the two orderlies could do not to laugh out loud.

27

They bound Xaviar securely and deposited him in a Viper, simultaneously awaking the little girl and removing her.

When they returned to where Jamie was keeping Guidry busy talking, they turned the girl over to the American officer.

"Take good care of her, Colonel," said Troy.

"What?" he said. "You're leaving me with a child in the middle of enemy territory?"

"You'll be all right," said Jamie. "By eight hours from now, there won't be a German soldier within two hundred miles of here."

"What are you talking about?"

"It's almost sunset," said Jamie. "That means you're just a few hours from June 6, 1944."

"So what?" asked Guidry.

"Tomorrow is D-Day," said Jamie. "The greatest military invasion in history will be in full flow before daybreak. The Germans will transfer every officer and infantryman they have to Normandy."

"Normandy?" he repeated unbelievingly. "No one's crazy enough to land in Normandy."

"Let's just say that no one's crazy enough to anticipate it," said Jamie with a smile.

"The trains to the concentration camps aren't

135

scheduled to leave until tomorrow morning," added Troy. "So if you just wait until the Nazis have left the area, you can probably free all the Jewish prisoners and reunite this little girl with her family without firing a shot. Then just march them to the sea. I guarantee the Germans will be otherwise occupied."

"Isn't it about time I found out who you people are?" said Guidry, but without any aggressiveness this time.

"Colonel, give me your dog tags for a minute," said Jamie.

He did as she asked. She pulled a sharp instrument out of her pocket and scratched "WATERGATE—1972" on the back of the tags.

"Someday, thirty years or so from now," she said, returning the tags, "when you're showing your medals and mementos to your grandchildren, take a look at what I just did."

"Watergate, 1972," he read. "I don't understand. Is it an address?"

"Just remember," said Jamie.

28

The Vipers were visible again, their energizers having run down, but no one had yet discovered them. Troy pulled Xaviar out and stood him on his feet.

"You're all fools!" he said wildly. "I could have saved mankind, and you ruined my opportunity!"

"It's hard to save mankind when you begin by killing millions who would otherwise have lived, Xaviar," said Troy.

"You're a bleeding heart, just like your grandfather!" snapped Xaviar.

"Xaviar, we're going to take you back and let the Council of Twelve decide exactly what to do with you. Dillon, untie him."

"If you give me any trouble," said Dillon, removing Xaviar's bonds, "I'll stun you and carry you to your seat."

"Oh, I have every intention of leaving this place," said Xaviar bitterly. "You three didn't exactly lend any lustre or credibility to my reputation here." He touched something on his belt. "Yes, I'm leaving here—but not with you! I wish you all good luck—and good hunting!"

With that he vanished. Troy and Dillon dove through the air, hoping to make contact with him, but all they managed to do was collide with the sound of Xaviar's mocking laughter.

137

"Why not blanket the area with your stun ray, or whatever you call it?" asked Jamie.

"Because if he's hit by it, there's no guarantee we could find him before some Germans wandered over this way. And we can't afford to let the invisibility field fall into their hands if they stumble across him before we do," said Troy. "How did he get his hands on a field, anyway?"

"My fault," said Dillon. "I removed your controls when you were wounded, since they didn't work anyway. I guess he found them and fixed them."

"Even with his hands tied?" asked Jamie.

"He's a brilliant man, Jamie," said Troy, "even if he is a bit unbalanced. He had the freedom to maneuver his fingers, and he had about ten minutes to work."

"But you had longer than that and couldn't fix it," she protested.

"I'm a warrior," said Troy. "Xaviar's one too, of course, but he's also a scientist, or at least a technician."

"So what do we do now?" she asked.

"We tell Adama that history is unchanged but Xaviar is still on the loose," said Dillon.

"There's an old expression where I come from to describe a situation like this," said Jamie. "The operation was a success, but the patient died."

Nobody laughed.

Part 3:

SOON

29

And so they are back, and the operation was a mixed success.

And yet, to my amazement, a number of our people think that Xaviar had the right idea, that it is just and proper to go back into Earth's past and change things, advance things.

Of course, they say that they wouldn't help people like the Nazis or the Inquisitors; they'd only help the sides that fought for the right . . . and I cannot make them understand that this is just as wrong.

Stop Germany from becoming a major power again for World War Two and you may kill off an Einstein, a von Braun, a Willy Ley—for all three men emigrated, and all three might have been killed instead had the English and the French been given better weapons at the beginning of the 20th Century.

Even a seemingly little thing, like helping the Americans win independence a little earlier against the British, has vast and unforeseen consequences. Give them a "super weapon" and John Adams won't have to bully the Continental Congress into debating the wisdom of fighting for independence, and as a result Thomas Jefferson won't have to write his magnificent Declaration of Independence, and the United States may be formed along wholly different lines.

The Napoleonic Wars? Help the British and the map
of Europe would be a totally different thing; help the
French and the British would never produce a Gladstone
or a Disraeli or a Churchill.

Or, to use a more delicate situation, take the North
African theater during World War One. If we were to
aid the English, who were under the command of a man
called Allenby but whose fortunes rose or fell with the
magnificent warrior known as Lawrence of Arabia, the
Arab states today would be British colonies. If we
would have helped the Ottoman Empire, most Arabs
would be speaking Turkish today. Had we given our
technology to the Arabs themselves, they would have
driven Israel into the sea in 1947.

And yet, say those who would have us do these
things, who really cares if the Arabs speak English,
Turkish, or Arabic? If they can't come to our aid, there
won't be any of them left to speak in *any* language once
the Cylons discover them. According to their arguments, and some credence must be given to them, it is
better to change Earth's history, to even end (or cause
never to happen) a few million lives, in order to bring
Earth's technology and weaponry up to our own level—
because the alternative is the total destruction of the
Earth by the Cylon fleet, if not now, in a few years or a
century. And Doctor Zee does confirm that Earth,
under its present rate of development, won't be ready to
withstand the Cylons for another seven or eight centuries.

And always is the memory that *we* had colonies and
battlestars that were capable of defending themselves
from the Cylons, and all that remains of them is the
Galactica.

The people who propound these views are not half-
crazed reprobates like Xaviar. They're good, decent
men and women who feel that this is the only way to
save either Earth or ourselves. Thus far Doctor Zee and
I have carried the vote of the council, but how much
longer we can do so I do not know.

And, speaking of Xaviar, where is he?

My grandson thwarted him in 1944, but he is still on the loose, traversing the corridors of Time with but a single thought: to hasten Earth's power to destroy before her citizens are ready for such power. A needle in a haystack is far easier to find than a single madman in a timestream. For once we begin looking for him again, we must not only pinpoint the When of his plans, but also the Where. Earth isn't a very big planet, astronomically speaking, but it's quite big enough for a single man to hide on.

So Doctor Zee continues to monitor all aspects of Earth's daily life: its maps, its weaponry, its news reports, its religions, its technology, looking for a change, a clue that will point out that Xaviar has been tinkering with the past, speeding things up abnormally.

As for my grandson, I heard his debriefing sessions with Doctor Zee, and words cannot express the pride I feel. It is true that Xaviar is still at large, but the things that Troy accomplished, the split-second decisions that he had to make, the privations he underwent at the hands of the Nazi barbarians, the fact that history did remain unchanged . . . words fail me.

Truly, he is Boxey no longer. And I know that Apollo would have been as proud of Captain Troy as I am.

Lieutenant Dillon, too, comported himself with honor and distinction. I must confess that I used to have my doubts about him. He's not as quick to grasp all the subtleties of a situation as Troy, and he was always too eager to charge into action, lasers blazing, without first considering all the ramifications of his actions. He is still reminiscent of what Jamie Hamilton calls a bull in a China shop, but most of the rough edges have been smoothed away, and he has my highest commendations for his actions on his trip to the past.

Jamie Hamilton was probably the key. She was able to advise Troy and Dillon on certain customs and procedures, and I truly doubt that they would have prevented Xaviar from accomplishing his goals without her help. Also, based on the debriefing sessions, she was willing to place herself in mortal danger on more than one occasion, and her courage was unquestionably as much an asset to our two warriors as was her knowledge.

Indeed, she would have made a fine Galactican—but why not? She is a fine Earthling, and what, really, is the difference?

30

Xaviar strode aimlessly through the streets of down-town Los Angeles, debating his next move.

He still had the invisibility field, of course; and he had a small arsenal aboard his Viper, which was hidden in an abandoned barn out at the edge of the Mojave Desert.

But what he didn't have was a power base. He couldn't return to the *Galactica*'s library tapes to find out what he needed to know, and there was no feasible way of replenishing his ammunition when he ran out.

In fact, he wasn't sure what he was doing here in 1980, a few weeks after he had departed for the World War Two era. Certainly he was no more familiar with the customs of Los Angeles in 1980 than he had been with Obersalzberg in 1944, and while he naturally spoke the language with perfect enunciation, he knew he would be woefully inadequate in coping with slang and colloquialisms for a few days.

Probably, he decided, it was because the *Galactica* was here in this era. Adama and his crew were his mortal enemies now—but they were also the only familiar thing about this strange section of the galaxy, and he knew that if he got in serious trouble here he could always get the Galacticans to pull his chestnuts out of the fire simply by threatening to reveal his origin to the locals.

And if that didn't work, he decided with a grim smile, there were always the Cylons. He would threaten to expose Earth to them, and if Adama didn't sue for peace or truce at that point, he'd actually carry through with his threat.

Others had tried dealing and intriguing with the Cylons in the past, he knew, and had always come to grief—but he was no ordinary man. He was Xaviar, and neither Adama nor the Cylons were going to stand in his way as he sought—*what*?

What did he want? He examined his thoughts and emotions carefully, looked into the deepest recesses of his soul, and finally admitted what he had known ever since Obersalzberg: the *Galactica* didn't matter to him at all. He was no longer interested in the fate of his countrymen, indeed even of his entire species.

Oh, he wanted them to live. After all, what good is it to preside over an empire if there is no one around to know of it? But empire was what he was after, what he craved all the way down to the marrow of his bones.

Let Adama and Troy and Boomer and all those other bleeding hearts and do-gooders worry about the Cylons. He would live out his life in comfort—no: in luxury—and let future generations, if any, take care of themselves. Life could be good aboard a battlestar, especially one like the *Galactica*, but it could be even better with a city or a nation or an entire world at his disposal, with three billion bodies struggling to do his bidding.

He'd end the silly notion of democracy, of course. It only worked in peacetime anyway. The Council of Twelve was incredibly slow in its deliberations; if warriors such as Apollo and Starbuck and Troy and himself and even Adama had always waited for the council to tell them what to do, the Cylons would have destroyed them a dozen times over. He and he alone would make all decisions, and his first decision would be which women (he had already abolished the notion of monogamy, in his mind) he would choose to have his children and thus make certain that the Xaviar line would not perish.

Another thing he would do would be to give his subjects the power of interstellar, or possibly even intergalactic, flight. Then, rather than trying to defend this mudball of a planet, they would swarm out to the stars, setting up a hundred, a thousand, new colonies of humanity—each to be ruled, of course, by one of his sons or daughters.

But when to begin? (Make that a capitalized When, he amended.) Ancient Rome? Da Vinci's Renaissance? Stalin's Russia? The America of 1980?

He didn't know. He was convinced that he would have an easier time of it if he took over a totalitarian state, since free men usually relinquished their liberty with the greatest reluctance . . . but he also knew that the first duty of political power was to perpetuate itself, and it would be much more difficult to infiltrate and ultimately take possession of the power structure of a totalitarian state than a democracy. After all, totalitarians preserved themselves; democrats only preserved their political systems.

And he could make a democratic system work for him. Man was not a social or a political animal, as Adama thought, but a competitive animal. The elective process was built around this competitive urge, channeled it into useful directions, and with his technology and the psychological breakthroughs that had been made among his people over the eons, he would have an enormous competitive edge. After it was over, after he had taken power legally, that would be the proper time to do away with the system. Hitler was a primitive, hampered by his technology and a streak of madness, but he had been on the right track. Xaviar openly approved of the man and his methods; he just didn't like the results—but Xaviar was no Hitler, and *his* results would be a lot better.

There were a few obstacles to overcome, to be sure. Adama's grandson, for one. Troy and his idiot companion, Dillon, would be after him again before long, once that disgusting teenaged mutant aboard the *Galactica* pinpointed his location in Time and Space, and he would have to be ready for them. He had escaped in Germany, but that had been through a stroke of luck, and Xaviar didn't like to count on luck.

This time he would need an ally, someone who would help him maneuver his way through the customs and mores of late 20th Century America, someone with the vision to see the dynasty that Xaviar planned to build. He would be well rewarded for his loyalty and his aid—at least as long as he was useful. After that, well, what was one aide more or less?

But who should this ally be?

Simple: who had Troy and Dillon gotten in touch with? Who would be ready to accept him for what he was?

Not the girl they had in Germany, that was for sure. They'd already had time to thoroughly brainwash her; she wouldn't be willing to change sides now, not even to join a sure winner like himself.

Then who else?

Mortinson!

The Nobel Prize winner. He'd have a mind, too. He'd know who Xaviar was, and he'd probably know about the Cylons, and he wouldn't have had much time alone with Troy and Dillon, so he could easily be swayed.

Easily? Well, there were ways and then there were ways, and Xaviar had means of persuading people who did not wish to be persuaded.

And, unable to separate fantasy and reality in the confused passageways of his brain, Xaviar set off to find Doctor Alfred Mortinson.

31

The Vipers touched ground, and Troy and Dillon immediately hit the switches that activated the invisibility fields.

"I wish we'd remembered to bring two more turbo bikes," said Dillon as he helped Jamie out of the Viper.

"Just be glad Adama let us come at all," said Troy. "He was furious when he found out that we had to leave the last two bikes behind. I really think if he'd known about that before we went to Germany, he wouldn't have let us go."

"Can our military experts learn much from the bikes?" asked Jamie.

"Not in a practical sense," said Troy. "As I've said before, we don't operate along strict Einsteinian principles, so even if they take them apart piece by piece they won't discover the motive power, not the way their thinking has been shaped. And once they've been taken apart, they'll never be able to put the motors back together properly. But from a broader viewpoint, they can learn one very important thing: that no one on Earth could have constructed those bikes."

"Not that they'll be able to do anything about it," said Dillon.

"Don't bet on it," said Troy grimly. "There's always Xaviar to consider."

"I don't know," said Dillon. "We managed to get so

many people on our tails the last time we came down here that if he admits he's one of us, I think he'll stir up more trouble than he can handle.''

"Don't underestimate him," said Troy. "Even with his hands tied, he managed to repair the field controls. And without knowing a thing about the period and its customs, he moved up to a position of power in the Nazi hierarchy in less than a month. He's a lot more dangerous than you think."

"Then the sooner we return Jamie and get on his trail, the better," said Dillon. "Watch this, Troy; I've been studying up."

He walked to a nearby state highway and stuck his thumb out awkwardly, a broad and ingratiating smile on his handsome face.

Seven cars in a row passed him by without slowing down.

"What am I doing wrong, Jamie?" he said at last. "It worked on one of your commercial transmission bands."

"Why don't you fellows stand back and let me take a crack at it?" said Jamie, stepping up to the side of the road. A car came into view about half a mile away, and Jamie slid her skirt up to her thigh and extended her thumb.

The squeal of the brakes were deafening.

"Nothing to it," grinned Jamie.

They rode to a truck stop and thanked the driver as he pulled off the road.

"What kind of place is this?" asked Dillon.

"A truck stop," said Jamie. "It's where the drivers of these big vehicles stop to eat and service their trucks."

"I wonder if they can do anything for a space vehicle with a low energizer?" said Troy, wondering how long the invisibility screen would hold up this time.

"You're kidding, right?" said Jamie.

"Certainly."

"Well, don't," she said. "I have enough trouble understanding you guys when you're being serious."

They walked to a table and Dillon picked up a menu.

"Coffee?" he said, staring at the writing. He checked his wrist computer. "A beverage derived from a bean, generally served hot. Troy, they drink beans here."

"You think that's weird?" said Troy, perusing his own menu. "They make a sandwich called a hamburger that has no ham in it, and they've got a dish called chili that's served hot instead of cold. What's a sandwich anyway, Jamie? It sounds like it's loaded with powdered silicon."

"It's a meal . . . no, a dish . . . well, it's something to eat that comes between two pieces of bread, or reprocessed and cooked bread dough shaped like a bun . . . and it can be meat or cheese or any number of things . . . I'm not being too clear, am I?" she concluded lamely.

"What about the sand?" persisted Troy.

"It has nothing to do with sand. The concept was created by an Englishman named the Earl of Sandwich. It's his only claim to fame."

"You mean this guy just kept playing with bread dough and meat until it came out right?" asked Dillon. "What a way to make a living!"

"I don't think he exactly did it for a living," said Jamie.

"It's a very international restaurant," commented Troy. "English muffins, French toast, Polish sausage . . . and yet only Americans seem to patronize it."

"Those are ways of making and serving things," said Jamie patiently. "The toast isn't made in France, the muffins aren't made in England . . ."

"Very confusing," said Troy. "But interesting."

"What do you want to order?" said Jamie.

"Oh, nothing," said Dillon. "We ate a week ago."

"You're kidding me again, right?" she said.

"You told us not to," said Dillon.

"You mean to tell me you only eat once a week?" she said incredulously.

"Sometimes," said Troy. "We usually eat two or three meals every day aboard the *Galactica*, but that's not always practical when we're aboard the Vipers. Too much weight and storage space needed for food."

"Look, sometimes I find it inconvenient to eat, too,"

said Jamie, "but I still have to do it."

"Doctor Zee has changed all that," said Troy. He scratched his head. "What can I liken it to? Ah, I have it! You have an animal on this planet called a bear. It hibernates during the winter."

"So what?" said Jamie.

"Well, when it's hibernating, its body uses only stored fat."

"Everyone knows that."

"No," said Troy. "What I mean is that the bear uses one hundred percent fat. No protein at all, nothing else but fat. Nothing provides as much energy or is used as efficiently. The hibernating bear has nothing to transform into urine or fecal matter, because the fat is completely efficient. There *is* no waste. And when he wakes up he's not a mere rack of bones; he still has plenty of fat left, because so little of it is needed. Doctor Zee has synthesized a catalyst that causes our bodies to act in much the same ways. I love food, and so does Dillon, but neither of us have eaten for a week, and our efficiency is unimpaired."

Jamie shook her head. "I love you two guys, but Lord, you sure take a lot of getting used to. Oh, well, let me get you a newspaper to read while those of us who are less fortunate, like myself, eat a little breakfast."

She walked over to a vending machine, put in a quarter, opened it to withdraw a paper—and froze. Then, recovering, she hastily picked it up and returned to the table with it.

"Look!" she said, holding up the front page. "We're wanted criminals!"

And indeed they were. Photos of all three were plastered across the front page in connection with the Mortinson "kidnapping," as well as the damage done to the Pacific Institute of Technology and the escape from the police.

"Not a very good likeness," said Dillon, looking at his photo. "It's not even in three dimensions."

"Stop it, Dillon!" said Jamie. "The police have an APB out for you two."

"What's an APB?" asked Dillon.

"An All Points Bulletin," said Jamie. "Don't look it up on that silly little computer. It means they won't take chances if you resist arrest. They'll shoot to kill. Do you understand what I'm telling you?"

"I think we'd better leave at once," said Troy.

"What will I tell the police?" said Jamie. "They think I'm in cahoots with you, that I was your inside man when you tried to kidnap the Doctor."

"Doctor Mortinson knows otherwise," said Troy. "He'll exonerate you. We've got to leave. It isn't safe here, and if you're seen with us they might decide to start shooting at you, too."

Suddenly the juke box, which had been silent, blared into sound, with a staccato drumbeat leading into a rock song. At the first sound of the drum Troy and Dillon leaped to their feet, their weapons drawn. A waiter who was carrying a tray in the vicinity jumped backward in stunned surprise and dropped half a dozen cups and saucers.

"Just joking," said Jamie weakly.

"What is that thing?" said Troy as he and Dillon sat back down.

"Just a juke box," said Jamie. "A music machine."

"I once had a personalized robot companion on the planet Pinta that looked very much like this," said Dillon. "Sounded better, though."

"I really hate to let you two guys go off on your own," said Jamie. "You just don't know enough. Like with the juke box. You're going to give yourselves away in five minutes."

"That's just a chance we'll have to take," said Troy. "We can't take you with us. After all, you have to live on this world. You'd better hunt up the authorities and get Mortinson to corroborate your testimony."

"We'll be in touch again, I'm sure," said Dillon, rising and walking to the door.

"I'll never forget you," she said. "Don't forget me."

"Not a possibility," said Troy. "Did I get it right?"

"Close," said Jamie. "It's 'Not a chance.' "

"Well, accept the sentiment," said Troy.

A moment later they were gone.

32

TRANSCRIPT OF UNITED BROADCASTING CORPORATION
INTERVIEW WITH NOBEL LAUREATE ALFRED
MORTINSON:

ANDERSON: Doctor Mortinson is in the United
Broadcasting Corporation's studios in Los Angeles this
morning, to talk with us about his ordeal. Doctor, a lot
of mystery surrounds your abduction and escape, and
the police imply that you've been less than helpful.

MORTINSON: I can't tell them what I don't know.

ANDERSON: For a man who was taken hostage, you
certainly don't sound very angry.

MORTINSON: Why should I be angry? The police
and news media insist that I was kidnapped; I insist that
I went with these young men freely and of my own will.
With all due respect to the police and to your fellow
journalists, I think I'm in a better position to know
what happened.

ANDERSON: Then perhaps you would care to share
your recollections with us. What, exactly, did happen?

MORTINSON: Two young men, whose names I'm
not free to reveal—

ANDERSON: They wouldn't be Troy and Dillon,
would they?

MORTINSON: How did you know?

ANDERSON: I have my sources.

MORTINSON: But I didn't tell any— Oh, of course.
They were arrested, weren't they?

ANDERSON: Could you please continue, Doctor?

MORTINSON: Well, these two young men—Troy
and Dillon—had something to say to me, something of
overriding importance. They came to my office and left
a message for me, a message which was a show of good
faith on their part and which was more than satisfactory
to convince me of their intentions. The police had
arrested them by the time I arrived.

ANDERSON: For breaking and entering.

MORTINSON: No. I think it was for illegal entry.
However, I refuse to press those charges, and the
Pacific Institute has also agreed not to prosecute.

ANDERSON: However, it's not up to you or the
Institute to decide. They broke a law, and now the state
will decide whether or not to prosecute.

MORTINSON: Perhaps, but they're going to find me
a very hostile witness. Anyway, I went to the jail to
make bail and found out that it had been denied. Since
they were wanted for no other crimes, I think this was
terribly unfair and prejudicial. At any rate, I met with
them shortly thereafter . . .

ANDERSON: After they had made a daring jailbreak, you mean.

MORTINSON: If you say so, Mr. Anderson. The
meeting took place in a car, and then we parted company.

ANDERSON: You neglect to mention, Doctor
Mortinson, that the car was going upwards of 110 miles
per hour through the streets and alleys of Los Angeles,
and that four police squad cars were in hot pursuit.

MORTINSON: What they had to say to me was
extremely confidential. We could not allow either the
police or the media to overhear it. *I* was the one who
urged them on to great speeds; let the police arrest *me* if
they wish, not Troy and Dillon.

ANDERSON: But you did have a representative of
the news media with you. Jamie Hamilton, a reporter
for our very own United Broadcasting, was in the car
with you. But neither she nor Troy and Dillon were in
the car when it crashed into a store, and none of the
three have been seen since.

MORTINSON: She was along as a friend of Troy and Dillon, not in her capacity as a reporter.

ANDERSON: Not so, Doctor. I was present while she was wired for sound just before she met with you.

MORTINSON: Did her hidden microphone do you any good?

ANDERSON: I must admit that it didn't.

MORTINSON: I believe you have your answer, Mister Anderson.

ANDERSON: But I have a lot more questions. For starters, what happened to the three of them?

MORTINSON: I don't know.

ANDERSON: Come now, Doctor.

MORTINSON: Really, I have no idea what happened. I must have been shaken up by the crash.

ANDERSON: Have you anything further to say before we return to our regularly scheduled programming?

MORTINSON: Yes. Our discussion was aborted by the arrival of the police and the press. It is my devout hope that I'll have the opportunity to see them again soon. My sole purpose in consenting to this interview is to make that point, should they be listening. Troy, Dillon—if you're out there, please contact me again. Don't worry about this gentleman and his cohorts; I know you'll find a way.

33

"Jamie!" exclaimed Anderson as she walked into UBC's executive offices.

He quickly ushered her into his private suite, then turned to his secretary. "Miss Davenport, see to it that we're not disturbed for the next half hour. Not a word to anyone about Jamie being here, and get Chief Modzelewski on the phone."

Jamie took a seat in front of Anderson's huge mahogany desk. There was a new photo on his wall, which would doubtless join the others in the outer office when he had a still newer one to replace it with. It showed Anderson and Doctor Mortinson, and unlike most of the other pictures, there was no inscription.

"You're lucky you weren't hurt," said Anderson, sitting down and lighting a thin cigar which had been smuggled out of Havana for a select clientele. "The cops are convinced that you were part of the attempt to kidnap the professor."

"The professor?" asked Jamie.

"Mortinson."

"He's a doctor," said Jamie.

"Doctor, professor—what the hell's the difference?" said Anderson. "They're all a bunch of eggheads. But this one's news, baby. Big news. The kidnapping has been on all the channels and in all the papers. Even

157

made *Newsweek* and *Time*, and I hear they're trying to get the guy who wrote *The China Syndrome* to script a TV movie based on it."

"But it wasn't a kidnapping," said Jamie. "It was you and the police who spoiled everything."

"Mr. Anderson," said a voice on the intercom. "Chief Modzelewski is on Line 3."

"Tell him I'll get back to him in a couple of minutes," said Anderson. He turned back to Jamie. "Jamie, I hate to say it, but you're sounding very sympathetic to the terrorists."

"They aren't terrorists," said Jamie.

"No?"

"No."

"Okay, Jamie: who do you think these two jokers are?"

"I can't tell you everything," said Jamie, choosing each word very carefully, "but basically, they are part of a worldwide organization."

"A spy ring?" said Anderson quickly.

"No," said Jamie. "It's what you might call a peace movement."

"And this is the way they achieve peaceful goals?" laughed Anderson. "By busting into buildings and out of jails, and by kidnapping innocent eggheads?"

"No!" said Jamie, her temper starting to fray about the edges.

"Are these guys some kind of religious freaks?"

"No. They're as religious as you are."

"I'm an atheist," commented Anderson dryly.

"Well, they worship some entities called the Lords of Kobol," said Jamie.

"Kooks!" said Anderson.

"They're intelligent, dedicated men," said Jamie. "You'll just have to take my word for it."

"Take your word?" repeated Anderson sarcastically. "I'm a *newsman*, for God's sake! We're not playing games here, Jamie. You were involved in a very serious felony." He softened his tone a notch or two. "Now, sometimes when men subdue a woman and take her captive, the law is willing to consider the possibility of brainwashing.''

"And only *women* can be brainwashed, is that what you're trying to say to me?" said Jamie hotly. "You think because I'm a woman I just swooned dead away at the sight of those big bold men? Well, let me tell you something, Buster: I've seen and done more things in the past month than you've reported in ten years. And another thing . . ."

Anderson was trying to hold back a grin of amusement when the intercom buzzed again.

"Mister Anderson," said the voice, "someone is trying to reach Miss Hamilton on Line 2."

"Tell them she's not here."

"He's very insistent. He say his name is Mister Dillon."

"Dillon?" said Anderson. "He's one of them! Put a trace on that call while Jamie's talking to him."

"No!" exclaimed Jamie.

"Listen, my intrepid girl reporter," Anderson said harshly, with his hand over the mouthpiece of the receiver, "you've got to learn to view this world from a wider perspective. These two men have apparently got some kind of hold on you, so I'm going to be recording this and monitoring every word."

He handed her the phone and nodded.

"Hello," she said hesitantly.

"Jamie," said Dillon. "Are you all right?"

"I'm fine. But why are you here? It's dangerous."

"It's Xaviar," said Dillon.

"What about him?"

"We just heard from Doctor Zee, who's been tracing his ship's electron emission—and Jamie, he's Here and Now."

"What do you mean?"

"He's in Los Angeles at this very moment."

"But why?"

"Well, if he hasn't tried to get to you, he's almost certainly after Mortinson. Can you help us warn him?''

"I'll do what I can. Now hang up and get the hell out of wherever you are!''

"Why?'' asked Dillon. ''You sound like something's the matter.''

"My boss has put a trace on this call! By now he knows where you are—and he already knows *who* you are. Hang up, Dillon!''

He did so, and she turned triumphantly back to Anderson.

"You shouldn't have said that, Jamie,'' he said severely.

"You're right,'' she said, as if an enormous burden had just been lifted from her shoulders. ''I lied to him.''

"You did?'' said Anderson, puzzled. ''How?''

"I told him you were my boss,'' she laughed, walking to the door. ''You aren't. You're my ex-boss, Hotshot!''

She slammed the door behind her.

It had a very nice sound to it.

34

Mortinson was relaxing in an old naugahyde recliner chair, puffing thoughtfully on his pipe and looking out over the rocky beach when he heard the door of his house open. He arose and walked toward the foyer.

"Who's there?" he called.

"A friend," said a low thick voice.

"Friends knock," said Mortinson, looking at the compact body and finely chiselled features of Commander Xaviar.

"Ordinarily I would have done so," said Xaviar smoothly, "but you *did* send for me."

"What are you talking about?" said Mortinson. "You tell me who you are and what you're doing here right now or I'm calling the police."

"I just saw your transmission, Doctor," said Xaviar. "You extended an invitation to us to continue our exchange of ideas which the police so rudely interrupted."

"Several million people saw that telecast," said Mortinson suspiciously. "Can you prove to my satisfaction that you're who you say you are?"

"If it's proof you want," said Xaviar, touching a small device on his belt and vanishing, "it's proof you'll get."

He reappeared on Mortinson's recliner.

"How did you do that?" said Mortinson.

"All in good time," smiled Xaviar. "This is just one of the things I can teach you."

"Why did *you* come to me, instead of Troy and Dillon?" asked Mortinson warily.

"They are outcasts, criminals," said Xaviar, "banished from our society. They came here only for personal gain."

"I find that difficult to believe," said Mortinson, who had developed an instant dislike of the man now confronting him, though for no reason he could put his finger on. "They gave me certain information, and offered to help our people."

"Of course," said Xaviar. "By duping a man of your stature and gaining your acceptance, they would find doors opened to them on every level of your culture."

"What kind of doors?" said Mortinson, cocking an eyebrow.

"Prestige. Power."

"I'm afraid you vastly overrate my importance," said Mortinson. "I pay my bills like everyone else. If I don't, they turn off my electricity, disconnect my phone, and repossess my furniture. I pay to get into Dodger Stadium, and there's no restaurant in the country that tears up my bill because of my status. I have a certain reputation among those who deal in nuclear power, but if you want to see what good it does me, come over to my office—if you can get past two thousand kids screaming obscenities and throwing rocks at the windows."

"You misunderstand me, Doctor," said Xaviar, rising and walking around the room like a caged tiger. His restless energy made Mortinson nervous. "Imagine how a fugitive from another world might live among you with his superior knowledge. You must pardon the comparison, but it would be like a man living among articulate apes. He could have anything he wanted."

"I suppose so," said Mortinson. "But even if what you say about Troy and Dillon is true, and I find it increasingly difficult to believe it, what can they accomplish now, with their photos in every newspaper in the county? That insensitive little bastard Anderson even has videotape footage of them meeting me outside the jail. If they're criminals in your society and in mine, where can they set up all this power and enjoy all this prestige?''

"They have a plan that includes traveling into Earth's past," said Xaviar.

"Is that possible?" asked Mortinson.

"Doctor, I intend, during the coming days, to show you just how possible it is," said Xaviar with a mysterious smile.

"Why would that be of interest to Troy and Dillon?"

"Have you an encyclopedia?" asked Xaviar, looking around the room at the book-lined walls.

"Yes. The *Britannica*. Just to your left."

Xaviar pulled out a few volumes at random and began paging through them rapidly.

"Look here," he said excitedly. "1777. If Lafayette and his French forces hadn't intervened at the Battle of New Orleans, the American Revolution might well have ended, unsuccessfully, within a year. They were out of money, Washington's troops were deserting by the thousands, the South was still unhappy with Adams and Jefferson even though the abolition of slavery was omitted from the Declaration."

"But why would that have been of interest to Troy and Dillon?" said Mortinson, repeating his earlier question.

"If they had secretly aided Lafayette and then sat on the sidelines for half a year, the American forces would be in total disarray and on the verge of surrender. Then they could have stepped in, won the war, and been acclaimed Presidents, Kings, or anything else they wanted."

"I find that a little far-fetched," said Mortinson.

"All right," said Xaviar, looking through another volume. "Ah . . . here's a more straightforward one. Caesar was killed—assassinated by his Senators—in 44 B.C. What if they had saved him at the last moment?

Between Caesar's gratitude and his appreciation of their weaponry he would doubtless have put them at the head of some of his armies—and the Roman Empire would have replaced the Republic half a century sooner. But with Troy or Dillon at its head, rather than Augustus.''

"You're serious, aren't you?" said Mortinson, his eyes widening.

"More serious than you can possibly guess," said Xaviar. "They could aid Napoleon at Waterloo, Lee and the Confederacy in the Civil War, they could replace Alexander or Genghis Khan or Charlemagne or Attila the Hun. The possibilities are endless. Their power would be unchallenged, for they wouldn't have to distribute it among their armies; their weaponry is quite sufficient for two men to defeat an army.''

Xaviar was rolling now, the words tumbling out of his mouth like water, his pupils dilated, his body in constant motion as he stalked around the room.

"Think of it, Doctor! They could rule the world, even the world of today, in a matter of a few years. Never forget the maxim: Any sufficiently advanced technology is indistinguishable from magic. They would be revered as gods, Doctor. As gods!''

"I'm suitably impressed," said Mortinson. "But why did they seek me out—and why are *you* here?"

"I keep telling you!" yelled Xaviar. "They wanted to gain your confidence!''

"What good would that do in the late Roman Republic?" said Mortinson.

"I don't know," said Xaviar. "Possibly you had information they needed.''

"They didn't have an awful lot of nuclear generators back then," said Mortinson, making sure he kept a few heavy pieces of furniture between them.

"Your library, Doctor!" said Xaviar impatiently. "By convincing you they were acting for the good of humanity, they would doubtless have gained free access to your library—and especially your volumes of history.''

"They could get the same from any public library,"

said Mortinson. He knew he shouldn't be arguing with this man, but he couldn't keep himself from pointing out the obvious.

"But they don't know how to use a library," said Xaviar. "They're completely unfamiliar with your customs. This was the easiest way."

"All right," said Mortinson. "Let's say, for the sake of argument, that I accept everything you've said. This still leaves a very important question unanswered."

"And what is that?"

"Why are *you* here?"

"To talk to you," said Xaviar, visibly trying to control his emotions. "To discuss the situation with you and find out the most likely historical eras where they might be hiding."

"I see," said Mortinson, finally piecing the situation together.

"Then you will help me . . . us?" said Xaviar.

"I'll have to think about it," said Mortinson. "After all, I—"

He was interrupted by the ringing of the telephone.

"Excuse me," he said, walking into the kitchen and picking up the receiver.

"Doctor Mortinson?" said a feminine voice.

"Yes," he answered. "Who is this?"

"Jamie Hamilton. We met at—"

"I remember," he interrupted. "What can I do for you?"

"Our two mutual acquaintances are in big trouble. A very evil man named Xaviar has escaped from their custody and they have to catch him before he does serious and possibly irreversible harm to Earth."

"Oh?" said Mortinson, unsurprised.

"Be careful. The man's a total maniac. And I think he's going to be trying to contact you."

"Absolutely," said Mortinson as calmly as possible.

"What do you mean?" said Jamie, quick on the up-take. "He's there, isn't he?"

The line went dead.

Mortinson turned and found himself staring into

Xaviar's cold cruel eyes. In the Galactican's hand was the end of the phone cord, which he had torn from the wall.

"It's a pity, Doctor," said Xaviar. "I'm a generous man. I would have rewarded you well for your help." He drew his hand weapon. "But I am afraid our partnership must come to a very premature end. I really don't need you any longer, Doctor Mortinson."

There was a soft hum of power, and Mortinson tumbled to the floor.

35

Troy and Dillon were waiting for Jamie as she stalked out of the United Broadcasting Building.

"What are you guys doing *here*?" she said, urging them to walk rapidly down the street with her.

"We don't have our bikes," said Dillon, "and we're still not conversant enough with your customs to hire a taxicab without taking a chance on exposing our lack of knowledge. Besides, we don't have any money."

"Did you get in touch with Doctor Mortinson yet?" asked Troy as Jamie stepped to the curb and hailed a cab.

"Yes," she said. "I'm sure Xaviar was there with him."

"What did he say?"

"Not much," said Jamie. "The line went dead."

"Please explain," said Troy.

"Just as he gave me the impression that Xaviar was in the house with him, the phone just . . . stopped. We weren't disconnected, because I called again and there was no ring."

"Perhaps he was outside," said Dillon doubtfully.

"You still don't understand," said Jamie. "It would ring even if it weren't answered, unless someone had done something to it. I even checked with the phone company, and they had no record of it being disconnected and no report from Mortinson of any malfunction.''

A cab pulled up and they got in.

"Any chance your boss will be following us again?" asked Troy.

"He's not my boss anymore," said Jamie.

"He terminated your employment?" asked Dillon.

"Uh-uh," she said, shaking her head. "*I* terminated it."

"What will you be doing?" asked Troy.

"I don't know," she admitted. "But after spending a few days with you two and seeing what you're up against and what you're trying to do, somehow all the work I've been doing seems to fade into insignificance."

"We can speak about you to Adama," suggested Troy. "Considering all the help you've given us, and all the help we'll still be needing, I'm sure we can arrange for you to come aboard the *Galactica* on a permanent basis."

"Hold your horses," she said quickly. "I'm not sure I'm ready for *that* yet. I've spent my whole life here."

"It was just an idea," said Troy, grinning.

"Horse feathers!" she grinned back at him. "You know I won't be able to resist it, don't you?"

"The thought had crossed my mind," he admitted.

They drove in silence for the remainder of the trip. The cab deposited them at Mortinson's front door and they raced inside.

The doctor was lying on the floor. He was just returning to consciousness when they reached his side.

"Are you all right?" Jamie asked, falling to her knees next to him.

"I think so," he said. "I feel like I've just gone the distance with Muhammad Ali."

"What's he talking about?" asked Dillon.

"He says he's sore," said Jamie sardonically.

"Where's Xaviar?" asked Troy.

"He's probably gone by now," said Dillon. "It takes more than an hour to recover from a stun. What was he here for, Doctor?"

"I'm not sure," said Mortinson. "Possibly to convince me to be his partner in crime, though what he needs with a nuclear scientist is beyond me."

"Bombs!" suggested Jamie.

"No," said Troy. "We've got stuff more powerful than any bombs yet developed on Earth. And besides, Doctor Mortinson doesn't make bombs. There are all kinds of nuclear scientists, current video dramas to the contrary."

"He also needed my library," said Mortinson. "I have the impression that he was interested in pivotal historical eras."

"That makes a lot more sense," said Dillon, helping Mortinson to his feet and leading him to a couch. "Jamie, could you bring him some water?"

Mortinson sat silently, rubbing his head, while Jamie poured him some water and Troy examined the bookcases.

"There are some volumes of an encyclopedia on the floor, but on the assumption that they're printed in alphabetical order, none of them seems to be missing. Could you go through your library and tell us what might have been taken?"

"Troy, that'll take forever!" said Jamie. "He's got tens of thousands of books."

"Most of them are scientific texts or works of fiction," said Mortinson. "I don't have more than 200 volumes that would have been of use to Xaviar. Let me take a look."

Dillon supported him as he got shakily to his feet and began walking up and down his bookcases, pencil and note pad in hand.

Twenty minutes later he sat down and handed a list to Troy.

"These are the missing books?" asked the Galactican.

Mortinson nodded, and Troy surveyed the list:

The History of the Decline and Fall of the Roman Empire, by Gibbon

A Stillness at Appomattox, by Catton

The Crusades, by Oldenbourg
The Peloponnesian Wars, by Thucydides
The Holy Bible

"That's it?" said Troy. "Just these five?"

Mortinson nodded. "As far as I can tell, that's all I'm missing."

"Well, this shouldn't be too hard after all," said Dillon.

"You think not?" said Jamie.

"Five books, five dates. Nothing to it," he said firmly.

"Except that the Peloponnesian War lasted for thirty years, the Crusades took more than a couple of centuries, the Roman Empire was around in one form or another for hundreds of years, and the *Holy Bible* covers about four millennia," she said.

"Oh boy," said Dillon softly.

"Well, I'm afraid we're going to need your services again, Jamie," said Troy. "You'll have to pick out the most likely dates for us to search for him."

"And the most likely locations as well," added Dillon.

"We'll leave you to your own devices, Doctor," said Troy. "I'm sure you can appreciate the urgency of the situation."

Mortinson nodded.

"Good. Then let's get going."

"Have you moved the Vipers?" asked Jamie.

"No," said Dillon. "Why?"

"Because I'm trying to remember which is the closest library to the route we have to take. I might as well check out the five books and start doing my homework."

"Good luck," Mortinson called after them as they walked out the door.

"That's exactly what we're going to need," said Troy grimly.

36

They decided to begin at the beginning.

"*The Holy Bible* goes further back than any of the other books," said Jamie.

"Who would you say is the first major figure?" asked Troy.

"Well, Adam was supposed to be the father of the whole human race, but Darwin's findings have proved this to be nothing more than a myth. I would say Moses, a Jewish prophet, would be the first figure of power."

"When did he live?"

"More than three thousand years ago," said Jamie. "And he survived for nearly a century."

"We can't spend a whole century waiting for Xaviar to appear," said Troy. "Can't you pinpoint the most important moment of his career?"

"He did so much," said Jamie, thumbing through Genesis and Exodus. "He accomplished fantastic things in Egypt and led his people through the desert to the Promised Land."

"How long was he in the desert?" asked Troy.

"Forty years."

"No good, Jamie. Xaviar can't waste that much time any more than we can. What single moment was pivotal in his career?"

"Probably when he received the Ten Commandments."

"What are they?" asked Dillon.

"The basis for almost all Jewish, Moslem and Christian law," she replied. "Supposedly Moses went alone to Mount Horeb, which is now known as Mount Sinai, and God delivered ten moral laws to him on a stone tablet."

"And the man who possessed the actual tablet would be in a position of enormous personal power if he chose to be?" asked Troy.

"I suppose so," said Jamie. "Not because of the commandments, but because he had spoken to God."

"When did this occur?"

"I can't give you an actual date," she said, "but I would guess it to be about 1275 B.C."

"It's as likely a place to start as any other, I guess," said Troy, setting the controls.

The old man with the long beard and stern demeanor walked up a narrow trail to the base of the mountain. He carried a staff in one hand, and wore a tattered robe spun from sheep's wool.

"Is that him?" asked Troy from his place of concealment.

"How should I know?" said Jamie. "They didn't have cameras back then, you know."

"Who else would climb the mountain?" asked Dillon.

"Let's get back to the Vipers," said Troy. "It doesn't matter if that's Moses or not, or if he spoke to your God or not."

"Huh? Why?" asked Jamie.

"Look around you," said Troy. "An impoverished desert land, tribes of men who are incredibly primitive even by your somewhat lax standard, a worldwide population smaller than Los Angeles of 1980."

"I still don't understand," said Jamie.

"We're dealing with a power-mad lunatic, Jamie," explained Troy. "This won't do for him. Not enough luxuries, not enough servants, not even enough enemies.''

"I see your point," agreed Dillon. "Why leave the present at all unless he could find something bigger and better, or at least easier and better, back here?"

"By the same token, I think we can skip the Crucifixion," said Jamie.

"That was when Jesus was killed?" asked Dillon.

"Right."

"But why?" asked Troy. "Our readings of your transmissions tell us that there are more than a billion Christians in the world today. That's a pretty big chunk of people to have worship you."

"You don't understand," said Jamie. "Jesus died for our sins."

"How can a God die?" asked Dillon.

"That's too metaphysical a question for me to answer on the spot," said Jamie. "But you'll have to believe me: the theology of Christianity is based on the fact that Jesus, like a sacrificial lamb, was predestined to die on the cross, carrying the sins of mankind on his back. This was how the race of man was redeemed from its sins."

"Strange," said Troy. "Sounds like death-worship."

"You're wrong," she said. "But do you want a lecture or an opinion?"

"An opinion, by all means," said Dillon.

"All right," she said. "When Jesus died he had twelve disciples, and at the most another couple of hundred believed in his divinity. If Xaviar were to either take Jesus's place or save the real Jesus from crucifixion, there would be no basis for Christianity. The religion wouldn't develop as it did. And Jesus was a pauper who urged all of his followers to disperse their worldly goods to the poor. No life of luxury there."

"Are there any other major figures in the Bible that might appeal to Xaviar?" asked Troy.

"Not really," said Jamie. "Not based on what you think he wants. The Bible ends with the first century of Christianity, or the first few centuries anyway. Everything that came before Jesus is in the Old

Testament, the first half of the Bible, and though there were remarkable rulers such as David and Solomon, I think Xaviar will consider their kingdoms too puny for him—if you're right about Xaviar, that is."

"What about the other books?"

"Well, the Peloponnesian Wars came about seven centuries after Moses and five centuries before Jesus, but ancient Greece was the cradle of civilization in those days, in many ways more modern than most parts of Earth today. It gave birth to Socrates, Plato, Aristotle, and a number of playwrights whose work is still being performed."

"Who was the major figure of the time?" asked Troy.

"A man named Pericles."

"And his greatest moment?"

"No way," said Jamie. "He was a statesman, a philosopher, an orator, and a general. He had about two hundred greatest moments. In fact, it can be said that the Golden Age of Greece was entirely his creation."

"Then that's it," said Troy. "When did this so-called Golden Age begin?"

"Thucydides puts it at 457 B.C."

"Then that's our next stop," said Troy.

"Why?"

"Because if Xaviar shows up there, it'll be to replace Pericles before his greatness is known."

And, on the outskirts of Athens, they found Xaviar's Viper.

"Well, he's here," said Dillon. "But how long has he been here?"

"Easy way to find out," said Troy. "Let's go back another six months."

And, six months further back, the Viper was gone.

By a process of trial and error, they ascertained to within 24 hours when Xaviar would land. Then they stopped Time-jumping and waited for him.

He arrived on schedule, but his Viper's sensing

devices warned him that they were there and he was gone again before they could fire on him.

"Well, we blew that one," said Dillon grimly.

"Next time we'll have to leave the Vipers a goodly distance away and accost him after he gets out of his own ship," agreed Troy. "Well, Jamie, what's next on our schedule?"

"The Roman Empire," she said, "but it's like hunting for a needle in a haystack."

"In what way?" asked Troy.

"Well, in one form or another, the Empire lasted for almost a thousand years, first as a Republic, then as a full-fledged Empire the scope of which has never since been equalled, and finally as increasingly smaller states calling themselves the Empire and trying to hold off the Dark Ages."

"Whatever they may be," said Dillon.

"Who were the major figures?" asked Troy, trying to narrow down his options.

"There were so many," said Jamie. "There was Julius Caesar and Augustus Caesar and Trajan and Hadrian and Marcus Aurelius and . . ."

"I get the picture," said Troy.

"However, the first two aren't really in Gibbon's book," said Jamie. "On the other hand, enough mention is made of them so he'll be aware of what they did."

"Too big," said Troy at last. "We'll proceed to the next era and if anything seems out of kilter we'll backtrack."

"That would be the Crusades," said Jamie.

"And what are Crusades?"

"Holy Wars, on the surface of things," said Jamie. "Every few decades during the Middle Ages a Pope or a King would organize a Crusade to the Holy Land, which is now Israel. Ostensibly the Crusaders went to Christianize the heathen and hunt for objects such as the Holy Grail, but actually they were out for profit and especially for additional farmland."

"How many Crusades were there?"

"Three," she replied. "A fourth was proposed by

one of the Popes, and the history books show an additional four, but only the first three amounted to anything. And at least I think there's an obvious target here.''

"Who?''

"Coeur de Lion.''

"Who's that?''

"Richard the Lion-Hearted,'' she said. "Coeur de Lion means Heart of the Lion in French. He was King of England, the son of Henry II and Eleanor of Aquitaine.''

"Why did he bear a French name if he was King of England?'' asked Dillon.

"He reigned for ten years, but spent less than a year of it in England,'' said Jamie. "He wasn't a bad general, but he was a pretty lousy king. He certainly spent more time in France than in England.''

"And why do you think Richard is the key?''

"Because Henry had consolidated the various English baronies to form a single nation, and Richard inherited it. Then, in 1199 A.D., at the age of 42, Richard was killed, dying from an arrow wound in the neck or shoulder.''

"I fail to see what makes him so important,'' said Troy.

"He left no heir, and his brother John became king. John was so weak that in 1213 he was forced to sign the Magna Carta, a document that returned most of England's powers to the barons.''

"Then if Xaviar were to save Richard . . .'' mused Dillon.

"Richard could well live another thirty years or so, and would probably be uncommonly grateful,'' said Troy, continuing the thought. "It wouldn't take Xaviar long to get rid of Richard and back up his claim to a still-united England with a bit of Galactican technology. Jamie, I think you've got it!''

"Then our next stop is the Castle of Chalus, on April 2 of 1199,'' said Jamie.

They were airbound and time-bound a moment later.

• • •

Troy, Dillon and Jamie hid behind some bushes 300 yards from the castle.

"Everyone's where they're supposed to be," said Jamie. "I guess that means he skipped the Roman Empire."

"Figures," said Troy. "He didn't know where to go any more than we knew where to look for him. Would Richard be that tall fellow standing by the gates?"

"Too big," said Jamie. "Richard's probably the little brawny one by the horses. Yes, he has to be! See, he's got a crown on! In fact, the fellow by the gate might be Robin of Locksley."

"Who's that?"

"He was the basis for a famous legend about a romantic bandit named Robin Hood, who stole from the rich and gave to the poor," said Jamie.

"I don't know," mused Dillon. "They *all* look pretty poor to me."

"These are the Middle Ages," said Jamie. "These are the nobles and the knights. You ought to see how the common folks live."

"Troy!" said Dillon urgently. "Look at that man standing about fifteen feet away from Richard, looking at the top of the castle walls. It's *him*!"

"You're right," said Troy. "I wonder how long he's been here."

"Long enough to ingratiate himself into Richard's service," said Dillon.

"That wouldn't have taken long," said Jamie. "Richard started this Crusade with more than 100,000 men. Between a few stupid military encounters and mass desertions, he's down to about 3,000 men now. His whole army is on the plain around the castle."

"That would be perfect for Xaviar," said Troy. "A nucleus to build on."

"Keep your eye on the wall," said Dillon. "I'll watch Xaviar."

They remained in hiding, motionless for almost two hours. Then a lone bowman stood at the top of the wall and fitted an arrow to his weapon. Xaviar drew a laser gun at the same time and took aim—and as he did so, Dillon drew and fired his own weapon in a single motion.

An instant later an arrow thudded home into Richard's shoulder and Xaviar screamed in pain, dropped his gun, and held his hand. He looked in the direction the blast of energy had come from, saw Troy and Dillon racing across the plain toward him, and jumped on the nearest horse and spurred it off across the plain.

Dillon took another shot, missed, and suddenly Xaviar was out of sight, he and his mount obscured by trees.

"We'd better get back to the ship," said Troy disgustedly. "We can't catch him on foot. Maybe we can pick up an electron trail in the Vipers."

They set off for the Vipers at a trot, reached them within twenty minutes, and immediately turned on their sensing instruments.

"Got him!" said Troy, taking off before Jamie had settled herself into her seat.

"Me too!" said Dillon's voice on the radio.

"He's going forward," said Troy. "Damn it! Lost him!"

"These Vipers don't have the tracking power of the *Galactica*," said Dillon, slowing his ship as Troy did likewise. "But he's got to be going to Appomattox, right, Jamie?"

"I don't think so," she said.

"But that was the last book!" protested Dillon.

"It's just a title," said Jamie. "Appomattox was the courthouse where General Lee surrendered to General Grant to end the Civil War. But the decisive battle was known as the Battle of Gettysburg. General George Pickett led ten thousand men straight up a barren steep hill to try to storm the Union position. It became known as Pickett's Charge."

"Did it succeed?" asked Dillon.

"No," she said. "It was a bloodbath. He lost six

thousand men on what came to be known as Cemetery Hill, and the South went straight downhill from there.''

"So if they had won," said Troy, "the man responsible for it would have been in a position of total power?"

"He could have replaced Jefferson Davis as President of the Confederacy if he had wanted to," she said.

"And the date?" asked Troy.

"July 3, 1863."

Neither the history books nor the paintings had done it justice.

It was, simply, the noblest and most ill-advised military action ever taken. The Rebels raced up the treeless hill only to be mowed down by the Union artillery. For every Confederate soldier who fell three more raced up to take his place—until, at long and bloody last, there were no Confederate soldiers left, and the hill was covered with gray-clad bodies.

Troy, Dillon and Jamie looked sadly upon the scene from a distant hill as the South's best and finest young men threw away their lives.

"Could you have been wrong?" asked Dillon when the last gun had been fired, the last soldier killed.

"No," said Jamie. "This was it. If Xaviar had carried the day for the South, it would have been a whole new ball game. But look at those poor boys lying there; what army could come back after a slaughter like this?"

"Then where is he?" asked Dillon. "Could we have been wrong? Is he back among the Romans?"

"No chance," said Jamie. "This war couldn't have been fought this way, date for date and detail for detail, if he had gone to Rome. England was a Roman colony, and America was an English colony. *Something* would have to be different."

"Troy," said Dillon, "you haven't said anything. What's your opinion?"

"That we've just watched all this butchery for nothing," said Troy slowly. "You see, I've just figured it all out. *I know where Xaviar is, and I know When he is!*"

37

ADAMA: What makes you so sure you know where he is?

TROY: Because I know where he *isn't*.

ADAMA: I'm afraid I don't understand.

TROY: Look at it this way, sir. He took five books with him. The ancient lands and times of the Bible didn't appeal to him, as I guessed they wouldn't. The Greece of Pericles is closed to him now.

ADAMA: Why?

TROY: Because he did nothing to change the future, and therefore our past is the only valid one.

ADAMA: What does that mean?

TROY: That any time he goes back to Periclean Greece to try to change history, he'll find Dillon, Jamie and myself waiting for him—because in this timestream we *are* waiting for him, and he can't change that without going back even further, which he seems uninterested in doing.

ADAMA: It's kind of muddled, all this business with paradoxes. What happens if you go back to 457 B.C.?

TROY: We're already there.

ADAMA: I know. I mean, what if you go again?

TROY: I don't know. I've asked Doctor Zee, and even *he* can't come up with an answer. But it would be a paradox Time couldn't correct, and Doctor Zee says that while he doesn't know the precise outcome, it would almost surely be cataclysmic. But to get back to the subject, we can rule out Greece and the Bible for the reasons I've mentioned, and the Roman Empire was so huge and so long-lived that even Xaviar can't figure out exactly where to plunge into the timestream. He tried to make an impact in the Crusades and we stopped him. And then he didn't show up during the Civil War. That's when it dawned on me where he was.

ADAMA: And where is that?

TROY: He's on Earth right now. This minute. In the Present.

ADAMA: And what makes you so sure?

TROY: Well, he's run out of reference works, but of course that doesn't mean anything. He could pick up some history books just as easily in 1940 as 1980. The real reason is because of what happened in Greece and the Crusades.

ADAMA: You think he's quit Time-hopping just because you stopped him a couple of times?

TROY: No. I think he's quit *because we were waiting for him*.

ADAMA: Elucidate, please.

TROY: We don't know what order he visited the past in. It could have been Greece first, or the Crusades. The point is that it doesn't make any difference. Once we pinpoint where he'll be, it's no great problem to get there ahead of him. You see, the nature of Time seems to be such that the past of the Earth we see down there is immutable as long as we have the capacity to travel in Time. In other words, her entire history is being codified by Doctor Zee's library computers. Any time that history suddenly changes, all we have to do is keep going further and further back in the past until we find the cause of it. Even if you and I were to die of old age, others from the *Galactica* could keep going back. It might take a day or a year or a century of our time to hunt Xaviar down, and yet only a few minutes would have elapsed on his time scale. He can't win and he knows it. If he appears in, say, 500 A.D., it might take us half the time from now to Eternity to find him, but once we did we'd stop him—and in his subjective Time he would be stopped in the first five minutes. Do you follow me?

ADAMA: Yes! And of course you're right! He's got to be here in the Present. That's the only way we'll be unaware of his actions . . . or at least of their ultimate results.

DOCTOR ZEE: Excuse me for interrupting, but I have been monitoring your conversation, and have concluded that Captain Troy is absolutely correct. The only course remaining to Xaviar is to infiltrate present Earth society in his way, just as we must do so in *our* way. But, thanks to Captain Troy, we now have the advantage of knowing that he is back in the present, and we are able to start monitoring events to smoke him out.

TROY: Thank you, Doctor Zee. Have you any instruments that can be of aid to us?

DOCTOR ZEE: Not yet, but you may rest assured that the creation of such devices will occupy my full attention in the coming days. And now, perhaps you'd best complete the first part of your mission by seeing Doctor Mortinson one more time and assuage any fears he may have about the state of your health. After all, for all he knows Xaviar has killed you and his entire world will momentarily flicker out of existence.

38

"It's really you!" exclaimed Mortinson. "I can't tell you how relieved I am to see you again!"

He ushered Troy and Dillon into his living room.

"I've been very apprehensive, as you may well imagine."

"I can appreciate that, Doctor," said Troy. He told Mortinson what had transpired.

"Then he's still at large?" said Mortinson.

"I'm afraid so," said Dillon. "But at least we know he'll be staying in the Here and Now. We should have a fix on his Viper before too much longer, and that should effectively nail him to this Time-frame."

"But that's only half the battle," added Troy. "He's still a very dangerous man, and we're very possibly going to need the help of the handful of Earth people we can trust. We consider you to be such a man."

"I'm deeply honored," said Mortinson. "I don't know what I can do personally, but I'll certainly pass the word among my colleagues on both sides of the Iron Curtain. I imagine that sooner or later he'll have to make contact with someone in the scientific community."

"We hope so," said Troy.

"You speak as if there's a very unpleasant alternative," said Mortinson.

"There's the military," said Troy. "Most Central and South American countries, indeed most Third World nations in any part of the world, would be only too happy to accept his aid."

"I see," said Mortinson.

"However, he'll have to move very slowly and carefully," added Dillon. "He knows we'll be monitoring all major political changes, just as we'll keep tabs on all scientific breakthroughs."

"And now, my friends," said Mortinson, "I wonder if I might ask one very important question?"

"You want to know why we're here in the first place," said Troy.

"Yes."

"Doctor Mortinson, I'm going to tell you the truth, because I know I can trust you to keep silent on the subject, and because sooner or later Earth must know the truth, since Earth's very existence is at stake. Centuries ago, many millions of light-years from here, humanity went to war with the Cylon Empire. The Cylons' stated goal is the destruction of every last member of the human race, and I regret to say that so far they've done pretty much what they set out to do. Earth is not the only planet populated by humans—or, at least, it wasn't until recently. But through treachery and because of overwhelming numbers, the Cylons are winning the war." Mortinson's eyes widened as he began to feel the impact of what Troy was telling him. "While Earth dreamed on, unimaginable distances away from her sister planets, every other human colony was obliterated. We took to the spaceways, living in great space-going fortresses known as Battlestars. Once there were many of them. Now there is only one: the *Galactica*, which is my home. We sought Earth out not to bestow the miracles of our technology upon you, but in the hope that *your* technology and weaponry would be sufficient to hold the Cylons at bay. This, alas, is not the case, and I fear we have led the Cylons almost to your doorstep."

"And *that's* why you helped me with my formula,

and why even that madman Xaviar wanted to go into the past and increase our current knowledge!''

"That is correct.''

"How close are they?'' asked Mortinson.

"Near Barnard's Star.''

"But that's more than half a dozen light-years away!'' exclaimed Mortinson.

"A hop, skip and jump,'' said Dillon grimly.

"I see,'' said Mortinson. "Pardon me if I seem to be slow on the uptake, but this is a lot of information to assimilate in one sitting.''

"There will be more than one sitting,'' said Troy. "Our plans remain unchanged.''

"You mean to bring our technology up to your level?'' said Mortinson.

"At least,'' said Troy. "And possibly beyond it. There's no telling what an Einstein, or even a Mortinson, might be able to do with some of the information we can supply you. You'll have our help if we can count on yours.''

"You can,'' said Mortinson, rising to his feet and earnestly taking Troy's hand in his own.

"Good,'' said Troy with a smile. "And now let's take a ride to your office.''

"My office?'' said Mortinson. "Why?''

"I began writing a formula a few weeks ago,'' said Troy. "I think it's time for me to complete it.''

39

FROM THE ADAMA JOURNALS:

And so it has begun.

We journeyed to Earth to find an ally, and, in bits and pieces, we are forging one. With men like Doctor Mortinson working side by side with men like my grandson, I think . . . I *know* that we have a chance. Not a certainty, but a chance—and since we are Men, we'll make the most of it.

Somewhere nearby lurks the Cylon fleet. Somewhere, just a few thousand miles below my feet, the mad Xaviar is still trying to create an empire at the expense of our race's future.

And the Earth itself needs more than technology: it needs care, and love, and sanity. Men still fight their fellow men, nuclear weapons are stockpiled, the foolish and the frightened battle tooth and nail against progress, the atmosphere is fouler every day, the seas and rivers are polluted, and the race seems closer to the trees and oceans it came from than the stars it seeks for.

And yet there are good people among that race. There is Jamie Hamilton, who has joined our cause; there are Doctor Mortinson of America and Professor Khalinov of Russia and Rashid Tarid of Pakistan, to name just three of the scientists who are working with us; and there are men and women, hundreds of millions of them, people of good will who will adopt our cause as their own once our existence is made known to them.

So, although our enemies are within striking distance, although one of us threatens to undo our work, although Earth herself was not the salvation we had hoped for, the wheels of change and progress are in motion, and I, who should feel cheated and betrayed by Fate, am finally calm and satisfied.

For while we have not reached the Millennia, and we have not found a weapon or a people to use against the Cylons, and we have much to do to protect those whom we had hoped would protect us, yet we have set events in motion.

We have begun!